Goddess Girls

AMPHITRITE
THE
BUBBLY

Goddess Girls

AMPHITRITE
THE
BUBBLY

JOAN HOLUB & SUZANNE WILLIAMS

Aladdin

NEW YORK   LONDON   TORONTO   SYDNEY   NEW DELHI

ALADDIN

An imprint of Simon & Schuster Children's Publishing Division

1230 Avenue of the Americas, New York, New York 10020

First Aladdin paperback edition August 2015

Text copyright © 2015 by Joan Holub and Suzanne Williams

Cover illustration copyright © 2015 by Glen Hanson

Also available in an Aladdin hardcover edition.

All rights reserved, including the right of reproduction in whole or in part in any form.

ALADDIN is a trademark of Simon & Schuster, Inc., and related logo is a registered trademark of Simon & Schuster, Inc.

For information about special discounts for bulk purchases, please contact Simon & Schuster Special Sales at 1-866-506-1949 or business@simonandschuster.com.

The Simon & Schuster Speakers Bureau can bring authors to your live event. For more information or to book an event contact the Simon & Schuster Speakers Bureau at 1-866-248-3049 or visit our website at www.simonspeakers.com.

Book designed by Karin Paprocki

The text of this book was set in Baskerville.

Manufactured in the United States of America 0715 OFF

2 4 6 8 10 9 7 5 3 1

Library of Congress Control Number 2015908992

ISBN 978-1-4424-8833-5 (hc)

ISBN 978-1-4424-8832-8 (pbk)

ISBN 978-1-4424-8834-2 (eBook)

CONTENTS

1

Mermaids

Amphitrite

WHOOSH! SWISHING HER TAIL UP AND DOWN, a mermaid named Amphitrite sliced through the bright blue waters of the glittering Aegean Sea. Her arms moved in quick, smooth strokes as she left the cave she called home. She was off on a serious mission—to track down her missing little sister.

Thin rays of pale morning sunlight filtered down

through the water above her to sparkle off the golden scales of her tail and throw highlights into her flowing turquoise hair. Sea grass brushed against her now and then, and eels peeked out curiously as she swam past. Her eyes searched the orange and pink branches of the coral reef below. But all she saw was her own shadow moving over it.

"Halia! Halia, where are you?" Amphitrite called out frantically. A trail of iridescent bubbles trilled from her lips as she spoke.

She wasn't alone in her search. Her sister Thetis was swimming right in front of her. Both mergirls were twelve years old. Although they were twins, the two of them looked nothing alike.

With a *swish-swoosh* of her orange tail, red-haired Thetis glanced back at Amphitrite over her shoulder. "Try not to worry too much," she said calmly, her words making bubbles also. "Halia's been lost before. We'll find her. And we'll probably all be back in time for MUMS, I bet."

Mediterranean Undersea Middle School, she meant. Their school had taken its name from a larger sea just south of the Aegean. And today was Monday, a school day.

"Yeah, but she's never been lost for this long," Amphitrite fretted. Halia had gone shell-collecting yesterday and hadn't returned. With fifty mergirls in their busy family, her absence hadn't been noticed until a few minutes ago.

Officially, their family were all Nereids, the name for merpeople that lived in saltwater seas. They also had many cousins, though. Their Naiad cousins dwelled in freshwater seas, the Dryads in trees, the Oceanides in rain clouds, and the Lampiades in the Underworld.

As the two oldest mergirls in the Nereid family, Amphitrite and Thetis were responsible for keeping track of their little sisters. Which was like herding the great colonies of seals that their dad, Nereus, was in charge of. So difficult, it was practically impossible!

"The last time anyone saw Halia was in Shipwreck Bay. Let's try there," Thetis called back to her. The speed with which she shot forward indicated that she was more worried than she let on.

"Right behind you!" Amphitrite shouted in return.

As they set off for the bay, the mersisters dove deeper, disturbing the seaweed that grew on the ocean floor, so it danced and waved at them like long green fingers. To keep from being swept away by currents caused by the girls' passage, seahorses curled their cute little tails around strands of kelp and clung tight. A school of blue-and-orange parrotfish headed toward the mergirls, but then darted in another direction to avoid a collision.

Halfway to the bay, the sisters passed a busy construction site where a school of guppies was working on a decorative wall mosaic, each pushing a bit of sparkly, colorful shell into place. When finished, one day this site would be a gift from all water-dwelling creatures to their favorite god.

However, Amphitrite and Thetis were too anxious to pay much attention to what the guppies were doing as they propelled themselves through the water, pushing forward with strong strokes of their tailfins and arms. Soon they could see brighter bursts of sunlight dancing above them as the water became shallower. The bay was dead ahead.

The surrounding sea was lighter here—the same pale turquoise color as Amphitrite's hair. The water's surface was smooth as glass, but in stormy weather it could become wild and unsafe. Huge craggy rocks of black granite lurked in this bay, anchored deep in its rippled white sand floor. During school field trips, the girls' classes had explored numerous old shipwrecks, which these very rocks had caused in times past.

Amphitrite trailed Thetis, slipping among the rocks to trace a familiar path through the bay. Merpeople had nicknamed them "sunning rocks." With individual names like Oyster Rock and Diving Rock, each was well known to the Nereid family. Washed smooth by the constant crashing of waves when the tide rolled in each night, they were perfect for hanging out on a sunny day to comb your hair, sing, or read.

You had to be careful not to sit on the rocks for too long, though. There were risks involved. For one thing, the principal of the school—their mom—gave demerits for being spotted by humans. Even worse, if you stayed out of saltwater for more than twenty-four hours at a stretch, you could become landsick or even die! Exactly what Amphitrite feared could happen to Halia if they didn't find her soon. She kicked herself higher and lifted her head from the water for a few seconds in hopes of spotting their little sister. But she didn't see the flash of Halia's lavender scales anywhere on the nearby rocks.

Splash! Amphitrite plunged again and caught up to Thetis. "Up ahead. Over by Anemone Rock," Amphitrite told her sister. "That's where Erato said she saw Halia last when they were playing."

"Right. Okay," said Thetis. She sounded as breathless as Amphitrite felt. Their bodies were practically jackknifing now with their eagerness to hurry.

Finally, they reached the rock. With a mighty

flip of their tails, both mergirls surfaced. Water streamed from them as each planted their palms wide on Anemone Rock's slick, dark surface. With hard twists, they hoisted themselves out of the sea to sit upon it. It was still cold from the night, not yet warmed by the new light of the morning sun.

"There!" said Thetis, pointing. Amphitrite shoved back her hair, turning to look. A short distance away, among sand dunes just back from the shore, she saw a glint of shiny lavender. The same color as Halia's tail!

"Halia!" called Amphitrite. A few last bubbles floated from her lips to sail high into the air. *Pop! Pop! Pop!* Now that they were out of the sea and could breathe air, their speech wouldn't form bubbles any longer. She called out again, but there was no answer. It was dangerous to shout any louder. Mortals might hear them and come.

Amphitrite watched anxiously as Thetis chanted the shape-shifting spell that would allow her to walk on land:

"Legs from tail. Feet from fin.

Sea to Land. Change . . . begin!"

As her words died away, Thetis's orange tail transformed into legs, and her scales shrank into a cute orange scallop-design dress called a chiton. She leaped to her feet, then scampered over the rocks toward the sand dunes. Easy peasy. As if walking were as simple as swimming. Ha!

Since Amphitrite hadn't yet gained the gift of shape-shifting, she had to remain behind. Like a fish out of water—or more like a *mergirl* out of water—she could only watch in frustration and crane her neck to keep her sister in sight.

Sometimes she wondered if she would ever know

what it was like to travel by land instead of by sea. Would she wind up like her mermortal mom, a half-mortal half-mermaid, who'd never acquired the ability to shape-shift? Luckily, although their mom lacked any magical abilities at all, she'd earned a high status in the mer community. As principal, she pretty much ran the school.

Still, with all her heart, Amphitrite hoped she'd gain the power to shape-shift one day soon. Perhaps that was selfish, but she longed to see the world. As much as her dad would allow her to, anyway.

In less than a minute, Thetis reached the spot where they'd seen the flash of lavender. Amphitrite hugged herself to calm her fears as she watched Thetis kneel in the tall dune grass. She appeared to be trying to wake up their little sister. If Halia had been there since yesterday, she'd have landsickness by now. But it hadn't been anywhere near twenty-four hours since she'd left their watery home. So the case should be a mild one, right?

Only why was Thetis taking so long? Growing more worried by the second, Amphitrite inched her way across the rock to try to get a better view.

"Ow!" she yelped as she accidentally sat on a pebble. Scooching over, she saw it was actually a pink pearl. One that must've washed up onto the rock from an oyster shell during the night.

She picked it up and examined it. "I wish you were a wishing pearl," she told it. "Only, if you are, that wasn't my actual wish," she added quickly.

There was an ancient legend among the merpeople that told of the existence of a special, enchanted strand of magical pearls that could grant your fondest wish as long as you possessed it. Plenty of mortal sailors and merpeeps had spent their whole lives looking for it. No one had found it, though. In fact, nobody knew if it really existed. Not to mention what it looked like. For instance, how long it was or what color the pearls were. Still, whenever she found a random pearl like this, Amphitrite always made a wish just in case it might have somehow come from that special strand.

Squeezing the pearl tight in her fist, she murmured, "I wish I could finally make the shifting spell work, so I could go help Thetis bring Halia safely back."

Then her eyes went wide. "No! Wait! I should have wished for Halia to be okay!" Had she wasted the pearl on the wrong wish? It was too late to call her wish back. Each of the legendary pearls was only supposed to be good for one wish. She chanted the spell to see if her wish had come true:

"Legs from tail. Feet from fin.

Sea to Land. Change . . . begin!"

She stared hopefully at her sparkly golden tail for a few seconds. When nothing happened, her shoulders slumped. How disappointing! At least half of her sisters, including little ones like Halia and Erato, had already gotten the shifting gift. It didn't seem fair that the ability to shift still eluded her. She could really use it right now!

Amphitrite tossed the pearl into the bay. *Plop!* She gazed anxiously to where Thetis still kneeled. Although she was dying to know what was going on, she didn't dare shout again for fear of attracting the notice of any mortals that might be out and about this early.

If only she could be of some assistance. However, she had no choice but to watch helplessly as her twin sister picked Halia up and half-dragged, half-carried her over the dunes and back to Anemone Rock.

"Landsickness," Thetis diagnosed aloud, as soon as the sisters were reunited. That was obvious. Halia was breathing, but her skin was pale, lacking its usual healthy glow. Her eyes were shut and her head hung low, her arms limp. It was also obvious that their little sister had used a shifting spell to venture out of the sea. Her tail had transformed. She now had legs and wore an iridescent lavender chiton.

"We'd better get her back into—" Amphitrite started to say.

But she was interrupted by a shout. A whole family of mortals had arrived on the beach not two minutes' jog from Anemone Rock. And a large blond-haired woman in a flowered swimsuit was calling out to them through hands cupped around her mouth. "Is your friend okay? Need any help?"

"Oh, barnacles!" Thetis hissed in an alarmed tone. "We've been spotted. If Mom hears about this, we're dead." What she really meant was, they'd get demerits.

Amphitrite leaned around her sister, flashed a smile, and waved at the mortals. "Thanks, but we're fine!" she shouted back.

"Smile," she urged Thetis. "Wave. Look happy." That's what their sunning arts teacher at MUMS had taught them to do in such situations.

Thetis managed a bright smile as well and called out to them. "Just playing a game of, um, sea rescue!" She and Amphitrite began to coax Halia into the sea.

"Yeah," Amphitrite muttered under her breath as they scooted Halia over the surface of the rock toward the water. "So mind your own beeswax, mortals."

Despite the danger they were in, both girls giggled. But they stiffened when a cute little mortal girl with the family pointed at Amphitrite, the only one of the sisters sporting a tail at the moment. "Look, Mommy. A *mermaid*!" the child piped up.

Thetis stepped in front of Amphitrite to hide her from view, but it was too late. They'd been seen for what they were.

Amphitrite forced a bubbly laugh and waved toward the mortals again. "Isn't this mermaid outfit cute?" she chirped. "You can probably buy a fake mermaid tail just like mine at a shop in town. Well, see you!"

With that, Thetis pushed Halia into the water and jumped in after her. Amphitrite shoved herself off the rock and joined them. *Splash! Splash! Splash!* Halia sank between Amphitrite and Thetis, still looking lifeless.

Words bubbled from Thetis's lips. She was chanting

the reverse changing spell as the girls sank lower and lower.

"Legs form tail. Feet form fin.

Land to Sea. Back again!"

Instantly, Thetis shape-shifted back into a mergirl with an orange tail. Relief filled Amphitrite as the chant also worked on Halia. Although her change came more slowly, within a minute their little sister's lavender tail returned. She gave a small shiver. Her gray eyes blinked open. Then she grinned.

With a flick of her tail, Halia launched herself into Amphitrite's arms, then Thetis's. "I knew you'd rescue me!"

They hugged her back, both giddy with relief.

"You shouldn't have wandered so far. It was dangerous," Amphitrite scolded.

"You could've been discovered by a mortal," Thetis

added. "They might've taken you somewhere we'd never find you. You might've even died!"

Halia reached into her side tailpockets, which all merpeople had. When she withdrew her hands, she held a beautiful, perfect shell in each upturned palm. "Look what I found, though," she said in delight. "They're for sharing in shell studies class today."

Amphitrite and Thetis exchanged glances of frustrated amusement. Both knew that their scolding was useless. Their little sisters were growing up. Soon there would be no stopping them and their curiosity. When they began to venture onto land more and more often, the danger of them getting landsickness would increase.

Honk! Through the watery distance ahead came the low moan of a foghorn. Long ago, their dad had scavenged the horn from an ancient shipwreck and brought it home for their mom. Now she used it to signal the beginning and end of classes at Mediterranean Undersea Middle School.

"There's the horn! C'mon, hurry. Shell studies is first period," shouted Halia. With a happy swish of her lavender tail, she headed back in the direction they'd come, her landsickness totally a thing of the past.

Amphitrite and Thetis followed. "I don't get why some of our sisters are always wandering off," Thetis said as Halia swam ahead of them. "There's tons to do in the sea. Walking on land is fun once in a while, like a mini vacation from swimming. But who would want to do that all the time?"

"Me," blurted Amphitrite. Her eyes widened in surprise when the admission accidentally slipped out.

Thetis stared at her in surprise. "Really? Since when?"

"Since forever. I think it would be *crazy* exciting to

get to travel around and see the landworld." A little embarrassed now, Amphitrite gave a hard kick. Her silky turquoise hair fanned out behind her as she whooshed ahead of her sister.

Thetis quickly caught up and swam backward in front of her, eyeing her closely. "You mean you'd leave home if you could? Leave *us*? For always?"

"No! I—I was just daydreaming a little, that's all." Thetis's reaction was exactly what she'd feared and why Amphitrite had always kept her desire to explore the land that surrounded their seas a secret. She forced a smile. "I'd never really leave you and our sisters. How could I? I love you all *waaay* too much. Now, come on before we really *are* late!"

For Thetis and most of her sisters, the sea was enough. But the land would always draw some merfolk. Including Amphitrite. Her longing for excitement and travel was hopeless, though. And not just because she couldn't shape-shift. Her sisters depended on her. She'd never leave them. Not unless some magical miracle occured that would keep them safe without her help.

Her thoughts were interrupted when Thetis suddenly snapped her fingers. "Hey! Forgot to tell you. Dad got a special bulletin yesterday from Zeus—the King of the Gods himself. It said that the Temple Games will officially kick off at Mount Olympus Academy today. All schools, including MUMS, are to stand by for more news. And get this . . . there are rumors that some of *us* will be invited to participate in the games this year. Wouldn't that be *mer*velous? Dad said we should hear something more tomorrow."

A spark of excitement leaped in Amphitrite at this news. The Temple Games were a weeklong contest of skill, strength, and strategy. Like just about everyone else, she'd read about them in *Teen Scrollazine*. She and her sisters eagerly devoured each new issue of the 'zine as it came out. If any merperson wound up on the winning team, they would bring great honor to the realm of the merpeople. And they'd be in the news!

Just being *chosen* to be on a team would bring honor, Amphitrite thought. She'd love to be in the games. Then a sigh bubbled from her lips. Ha! Even if the rumors proved true, it wasn't likely *she'd* be chosen. She, who couldn't shape-shift. What use would she be to a team? No way would she ever be able to leave home and see the world.

Instead, she would have to act all happy for those of her family who *were* chosen. And she would be happy for them. But, oh . . . if only she could go too!

2

Choosing Teams

Poseidon

"STUDENTS OF MOUNT OLYMPUS ACADEMY!" ZEUS boomed. It was Monday morning, and he was standing at the top of the Academy's front steps, gazing out over the courtyard below. "The time has come to announce the official list of competitors in this year's Temple Games!"

Thirteen-year-old Poseidon, godboy of the sea,

whipped to attention at the rumble of the principal's voice. So did all the other MOA students standing in the courtyard. They'd all gathered there to await this very moment.

Behind Zeus, their school towered five stories high. It was built of polished white stone, surrounded on all sides by dozens of Ionic columns, and was perched atop the highest mountain in Greece—Mount Olympus.

Standing before the huge bronze front doors of the Academy, Zeus looked powerful and kingly. Not just because he was King of the Gods and Ruler of the Heavens, in addition to being principal of MOA, either. He was also seven feet tall!

And if all that wasn't enough to command everyone's attention, there were his bulging muscles, wild red hair, piercing blue eyes, and fearsome temper, too. Not to mention his skill at hurling thunderbolts to obliterate his enemies. Even if you weren't an enemy, sizzles of electricity would shoot from his fingertips and zap you if you were ever unlucky enough to make him really mad. (Sometimes, by accident, he zapped the walls and furniture in his office, too.) Everyone at MOA was a little afraid of the principal, including his own daughter, Athena. But they all respected and admired him as well!

Water dripped from the three-pronged tip of Poseidon's pitchforklike trident and ran down his arm. Realizing that he'd been nervously jiggling it up and down while waiting to hear if he'd made the list of competitors, he loosened his grip. He and many other MOA students had been practicing hard for weeks, all hoping for a chance to participate in the Temple Games. Still, he didn't want to seem too anxious.

Now Zeus lifted a scroll high in his meaty hands. Giving it a hard shake, he unrolled it. *Whap!*

Everyone leaned forward in anticipation.

The hambrosia and eggs Poseidon had eaten for breakfast a few minutes ago suddenly lodged liked a lump in his stomach. His heart pounded. His muscles tensed. The list Zeus held could change everything for him. In fact, this announcement could change his whole life.

Immortals and mortals alike probably thought he already had it all. Well, he didn't.

Sure, he was one of the most popular gods at the Academy. Sure, girls adored him. He was always getting fan letters from mortal girls on earth, and more than one girl at the Academy had crushed on him too. And, sure, he scored mostly As in his classes, and he ruled the seas. But, even so, there was one thing missing from his life. And being chosen as a team captain in these games would be the first step toward getting it.

As Zeus cleared his throat, a hand clapped Poseidon on the shoulder, startling him. "Hey, god-dude, what up? You just went from your usual turquoise color to green," kidded Ares. This blue-eyed, blond-haired godboy of war liked to tease. He could even be something of a bully at times, though his goddessgirl crush Aphrodite had gotten him to tone down that aspect of his personality lately.

Poseidon's eyes shifted to Apollo and Hades, who were standing behind Ares. They were also immortals. Apollo was godboy of truth, prophecy, and music, and was an excellent archer like his twin sister, Artemis. And Hades was the ruler of the Underworld.

For the benefit of all three guys, Poseidon gave

a relaxed shrug. "Nothing's up. Just kind of tired, that's all."

Overhearing, a mortal boy named Heracles, who was even more heavily muscled than Ares, came over. He carried an enormous knobby club against one shoulder and wore a lion-skin cape. "I know what you mean," he volunteered cheerfully. "Couldn't sleep last night, wondering if I made the list."

"Actually, I was hanging out at the Supernatural Market till late," Poseidon said quickly. Even to his friends, he couldn't bring himself to admit how desperately he wanted to make the list of competitors, and be made captain of one of the teams.

"Shh! Listen up, you guys," said Apollo, nodding toward Zeus. A staff member had interrupted the principal just as he'd been about to speak, but now he appeared ready to continue.

"We're doing something a little different this year," Principal Zeus began with a wide grin. "Going to shake things up. In the past we've sent seven five-member teams from MOA to compete against one another in games at various temples. This year, I have chosen seven team captains from among you, but assigned only two MOA students to each captain's team."

Murmurs filled the courtyard. Poseidon wasn't sure what to make of this change. Did that mean teams in the games would only have three members each? Why so few?

But then Zeus explained, his booming voice silencing all other conversation. "In the interest of encouraging friendly cultural relations with other lands, our seven captains will each choose two non-MOA competitors to also join their team. Which will make a total of five members on a team, including the captain, as usual. So to be clear, that's seven teams of five students each. A total of thirty-five participants drawn not just from MOA, but from around the world. Got it?"

He shot a glance at the students, who had begun to murmur again. Abruptly, they quieted, all nodding. "The seven team captains whose names I am about to announce were chosen from a list of those who requested the position," Zeus reminded everyone. "Please hold your applause until all seven names have been read."

"The captains who will represent the Academy in the Temple Games are . . . ," he began. Then he stopped to take a dramatic pause, eyeing his audience. Finally he continued, naming names at last. "Apollo, Ares, Artemis, Athena, Iris, Medusa, and . . . Pheme!"

Huh? A dozen emotions filled Poseidon all at the same time. But the one taking up the most space was mega-extreme disappointment. He wanted to throw up. He hadn't made captain? How could that be? Just like the chosen ones, he had been diligently practicing his skills on and off the sports fields for weeks now.

Everyone knew him to be a worthwhile competitor. It was a pretty sure thing that Zeus would now assign him to compete under the captain of one of the seven teams. But he didn't want to take orders from one of the other captains. He was born to *lead*. How had Principal Zeus failed to see that?

This just wasn't fair! Pheme had been chosen, and *he* hadn't? Really? Sure, she had wings. But other than flying, she wasn't athletic. And her grades weren't even as good as his. As the goddessgirl of gossip, her main talent was spreading news. She even wrote a gossip column in *Teen Scrollazine*. But those were hardly qualifications for the position of team captain!

The choice of Medusa made more sense. His eyes found the green-skinned, snake-haired girl. She wasn't an immortal and so hadn't been born with magical powers. However, she did have the ability to turn other mortals to stone with her gaze, which could come in handy against opponents in the games.

Since Athena had unintentionally given her this gift (or *problem*, depending on how you looked at it), she'd later invented special stoneglasses that allowed Medusa to control her stone gaze. Medusa was wearing them now. Instead of protecting against the sun, they protected mortals against being turned to stone by her stare.

"Remember, it's an honor to be chosen as a member of a team," Zeus went on. "Not everyone can participate, but there's always next year. Now, in a few minutes Hermes will arrive to deliver some scrolls that list the complete rules of the competition. Everyone here will get a scroll and—"

Suddenly the nine-headed Ms. Hydra, who'd been standing behind Zeus, stepped forward to interrupt him. Each of the administrative assistant's heads was a different color and had a different personality, such as her grumpy green one. She even had a pink head that was almost as gossipy as Pheme, at least when it came to news about Zeus.

But it was her gray head—her most efficient one— that whipped over to Zeus on its serpentine neck and whispered something in his ear. His bushy red eyebrows flew up in consternation. After a quick discussion with Ms. Hydra, he turned to address the students again.

"Sorry about that. I have just been reminded that Pheme will be going to the games in the capacity of reporter, not captain. Instead, the seventh captain will be . . ." He paused, thinking hard. Then he tapped his forehead and smiled. "I remember now. It's Poseidon!" he announced.

A thrill shot through Poseidon, replacing the horror that had filled him only moments before. He'd made the cut after all!

"Awesome, Po," Apollo said, mock-punching him on the arm in a friendly way. "Wouldn't have been the same without you in charge of a team."

"Thanks. I wasn't worried, though," Poseidon fibbed. "Knew there must have been some mistake. You guys need some *real* competition. Where would you be without me to provide it?" His friends laughed. But the truth was they all had amazing skills. Many variables in the games would help determine the ultimate winner.

When a metallic flash suddenly lit the sky, the boys all looked up. A beautiful silver chariot with mighty wings had burst through the clouds overhead. It was piled high with what looked like hundreds of six-inch wide white papyrus scrolls tied with purple ribbons. The driver was wearing a winged cap. It was Hermes, driving his Delivery Service chariot.

In an expert move, he swooped low, tilting his chariot sideways. *Boing!* A big coiled spring popped up from the back of his chariot, launching all the scrolls high in the air. After a few seconds, gravity caused them to reverse direction and rain down on the students. Then he nudged the lid off a box on the seat beside him. Seven purple papyrus scrolls, each with a pair of small wings, flew out. Without stopping, Hermes turned his chariot and headed off into the wild blue yonder again.

Down in the courtyard, hands reached. As the white scrolls were unfurled, students' heads bent over them to read the rules for the games. Before Poseidon could grab a white one, the seven purple scrolls magically winged directly to him and the other six captains. Seeing his name on the one hovering in the air before him, he grabbed it instead.

Ares was already unrolling the purple captain's scroll he'd gotten. "Look! These scrolls list our MOA team members too," he said.

Unrolling his own scroll and skimming down it, Poseidon found the names of the two MOA team members he'd been assigned. The first was . . . *Pandora*? Hmm. To tell the truth, if *he'd* been doing the choosing, she wouldn't have made his team. Not only was she a mortal, and therefore without magic powers, she was also annoyingly curious and might question every order he gave!

The second member of his team was Hades. Now that was more like it! Hades was his roommate and a stand-up godboy, too. In Poseidon's opinion, he actually had skills worthy of a team captain. And as godboy of the Underworld, a realm located below the earth, he could be a huge asset to the team if the competition happened to carry them there.

He had to wonder at Zeus's captain picks, choosing Medusa over Hades or Heracles, for example. But their principal put a lot of thought into such matters, and his decisions usually turned out to have been wise ones.

Everywhere around him, Poseidon could hear cries of excitement. Some who'd been practicing hard had not been chosen for a team. But they seemed to be doing their best to contain their disappointment, offering congratulations to those who *had* been chosen. Too bad there wasn't room for everyone in the games. At least he'd made it!

"Captains, keep your purple scrolls with you at all times," Zeus called out. "They are magical and will give your team helpful clues, instructions, and updates throughout the course of the games."

Before he could go on, Ms. Hydra's gray head slithered over and whispered something to him again. "Yes, yes, I was just about to get to that," he said. Then he addressed the students once more.

"As I started to say a minute ago, I have a special announcement for those of you who are not participating!" he told them with extra excitement in his thundering voice. He held up one of the white scrolls Hermes had delivered, gazing at it proudly. "No longer will you have to wonder what's going on during the games in faraway lands. Because with Pheme's help as reporter this year, news flashes about important events will magically appears on both white and purple scrolls all week, *as they happen*. At this very moment, Hermes is on his way to deliver more of these scroll-gadgets to rulers around the world so they can keep their realms informed too. I came up with this invention myself. Awesome, right?"

Looking quite pleased with himself, Zeus spread his muscled arms wide as if to say, *Ta-da! Isn't my scroll-gadget idea amazing?* A few seconds passed while he continued to hold out his arms, gazing out over the crowd expectantly.

"Clap your hands," Poseidon heard Athena whisper from somewhere nearby. As her advice spread, applause swept the crowd.

A satisfied expression filled Zeus's face. Smiling

big now, he called out, "So, listen up, team captains. By dinnertime tonight, you will need to notify Ms. Hydra in the front office of the final two team members you choose. She'll then summon them to meet you at the Delphi temple tomorrow morning where all seven teams will gather to receive some very magical information! *Good Luck!* That is all!" Turning on his heel, Principal Zeus pushed through the tall bronze front doors and into the Academy.

Ignoring the issue of choosing team members for now, Poseidon quickly skimmed over the additional instructions on his purple scroll. He saw that, as usual, teams would be given food to see them through the trip.

"'Look for the clay bowls decorated with black-silhouetted figures at each temple you visit during the games,'" Ares read aloud from the same part of the scroll Poseidon was reading. "'They'll contain your one meal of the day. Other meals must be scavenged from your surroundings as you travel.'"

Aphrodite came over to stand by Ares and silently study his scroll along with him. Artemis looked up from her captain's scroll and craned her neck toward Poseidon. "Who's on your team?"

Snap! Poseidon closed his purple scroll and grinned. "Wouldn't you like to know?"

"C'mon, we'll find out tomorrow anyway," said Iris. Besides being one of the captains, she was also the goddessgirl of rainbows.

"Yeah," Pandora agreed. "What's the big deal?"

"The big deal," Ares explained, "is that if we tell who our teammates are, other captains will have a jump on analyzing their talents. And on figuring out ways to cream other teams. If captains don't find out who's on whose teams till the last minute, there's less time to do that."

Aphrodite curled a lock of her long golden hair around one finger, then smiled as she let it go again. "Leave it to the godboy of war to be a few moves ahead of the rest of us in his thinking," she said. Her hair was threaded with curly ribbons and held back from her face with shell-shaped clips that matched her sparkling blue eyes.

Unlike many godboys at MOA, Poseidon had never been in like with her. But he had to admit she was startlingly beautiful. Which made sense, since she was the goddess of love and beauty. Most guys always seemed ready to help her, therefore her beauty could benefit Ares if she were on his team. Poseidon stared hard at her, wondering if she was.

Seeing his look, she easily interpreted the question

in it. "And no, I'm not on Ares' team. I'm not on any-one's team. Persephone and I helped Principal Zeus and Ms. Hydra write out the challenges you captains are going to face at each temple, so it wouldn't be fair if we participated."

A few minutes later, the friends drifted apart. Poseidon decided he'd wait till after dinner to tell Pandora and Hades that they were his teammates. They'd still have enough time to plan some strategy before nightfall. For now, he had some serious think-ing to do and not much time to do it.

Since team captains were excused from classes all week, he spent the rest of the day choosing the final two members of his team. He decided right off that he wanted them to be sea dwellers. That would benefit him in the end since it would bring acclaim to his realm. Plus, strong swimmers would be in good shape mentally and physically. At the Academy library he found a book that listed all sea creatures by name and gave brief details about them. Once he'd compiled a short list of candidates, he took it to the pool he'd built in the bottom of the gym, where it was quiet. He did his best thinking around water. And he wanted his two choices to be perfect.

After careful consideration, he chose one of the daughters of Nereus, the most respected merman in the Aegean and Mediterranean seas, to be on his team. Except for Nereus himself, merpeople weren't immortal like the goddessgirls and godboys who lived on Mount Olympus, but they weren't exactly mortal, either. They were somewhere in between, with limited magical powers.

He'd heard that Nereus's oldest daughter, Thetis, was skilled at shape-shifting and was being trained as a seal herder, too. Both could turn out to be useful skills, so she was his pick.

Also, choosing Thetis would put Nereus firmly on his side in the competition, Poseidon figured. And that would give him a definite advantage in what was already his strong suit. Because if Nereus caused any storms in the saltwater seas during the games, they wouldn't rage against any team his daughter was on!

His other choice proved to be a cinch in the end. He'd invite his childhood buddy, Delphinius. He could shape-shift into dolphin form and swim like a fish, er, like a dolphin. But he could also walk on land. His echolocation abilities could help with finding things. Plus, he was smart and loyal.

Satisfied with his decisions, Poseidon dropped off his two invitations at the front office just before dinner. Ms. Hydra's efficient gray head opened his invitation scrolls and scanned his two choices. "Good. No conflicts. We've had a few captains who chose the same team members and had to select alternates."

He'd been about to ask when the invitations would be sent out, when her impatient purple head preempted his question. "Invitations will go out via magic wind after dinner," she informed him. Thanking her, he headed for the cafeteria. He'd skipped lunch and was starving!

The godboys and goddessgirls at MOA ate ambrosia, a divine confection that kept them immortal. The cafeteria crew served it in many different forms, such as yambrosia stew and ambrosia salad. Ambrosia and the nectar they drank caused immortals' skin to shimmer. However, it had no effect on the few mortals who also attended the Academy.

In the dinner line, Poseidon chose ambrotoni, a

carton of nectar, and a couple of sides. "Here you go," said the eight-armed, octopuslike cafeteria lady as she handed him his plate. The kitchen seemed extra busy today, and the cafeteria lady looked frazzled. No doubt she had extra work on *her* plate due to the preparation of meals for the upcoming competition.

Poseidon gave her an encouraging grin. "Thanks!" As an afterthought, he snagged an Oracle-O cookie from a basket of them at the end of the line.

As usual, he ate his meal with his godboy friends. He gulped down his food super fast, saving his Oracle-O cookie for last. He was dying to ask it for a prophecy, but waited till the others took off for the tray return. Then he tore off its wrapper and eagerly bit into it. "Were my final two team member choices good ones?" he asked it, though he was confident the answer would be yes.

Instantly, a small, dramatic voice announced: "Thetis

could outshine you." It was coming from the cookie.

"Whah?" Poseidon stared at the remaining half, his turquoise eyes wide and his mouth full of cookie.

"Thetis could outshine you," the little voice said again in answer to his question.

"Whoa," he murmured, finishing off the cookie. That didn't sound good. He wanted skilled team members, but if one of them outshone him, the others might not accept his leadership. Plus, being upstaged could be embarrassing. *Hmm.*

The fortune cookies served in the MOA cafeteria were all made by a Trojan princess named Cassandra and her family, who sold them in their shop in the Immortal Marketplace. The cookies all talked, and their predictions were fairly reliable. (As long as they weren't *Opposite* Oracle-O's, that is.

Those cookies always predicted the reverse of what was true, but his wasn't that kind.)

Worried now, Poseidon leaped from the table. As he rushed his tray to the tray return, his brain frantically searched for an alternative to Thetis. On the list of Nereus's daughters, he remembered that Thetis had a twin sister. Amphitrite was her name. Since they were twins, she was bound to be just as good at shape-shifting and seal herding as her sister, right? Why take a chance on being overshadowed by Thetis? He would invite her sister to join his team instead. But he'd better hurry.

He dashed to the front office just in time to catch Ms. Hydra in the act of handing over the seven team captains' invitations to the magic winds for distribution.

"Don't worry," added Ms. Hydra's efficient gray head. "Since yours will deliver to the sea, I fixed things so they will transform into bubble-grams to keep them from getting waterlogged."

"Wait! I've changed my mind!" he shouted just as Zeus's assistant tossed out the last scroll.

"Too late. Invitations went out, as you can see," her sunny yellow head told him in her happy voice.

Poseidon could only stare as a flurry of eager winds departed with the letterscrolls carrying them to all parts of the world, where they would be read by those who had been chosen for the Temple Games. Including Delphinius. And Thetis . . . who *could* outshine him. Great. Just great.

Was it too much to hope that she might refuse his invitation? With a sinking feeling, he supposed it was. Everyone wanted to bring honor to their respective lands. Anyone he'd asked would probably have agreed to participate. If only he'd chosen someone else!

3

Invitation

Amphitrite

STILL SHOOK UP AFTER THEIR MORNING'S RESCUE efforts, Amphitrite and Thetis swam homeward behind their little sister. Halia had no clue what a close call she'd had with landsickness earlier, but Amphitrite and Thetis knew. All was well for now, though, Amphitrite figured.

Back at their cave home, the girls split up and

whooshed to their separate rooms to get ready for classes. Amphitrite pulled her spyglass from under her bed and collapsed it till it was small enough to fit in her net schoolbag along with other school supplies. Next she added an adventure story scrollbook from the MUMS library that she was currently reading for fun. Last of all, she grabbed her comb and tucked it into the pocket hidden among her scales.

Looping the bag's straps over her shoulders, she did a corkscrew twist that pushed her out of her room and back into the center of the enormous silver-walled underwater cave where she and her whole family lived.

In addition to her parents' room and communal gathering areas, there were fifty small bedrooms tucked high and low along the walls of the cave. One for her and each of her sisters. The rooms were really just alcoves that had been built in natural nooks along the walls, with beaded curtains they could close for privacy.

Each was labeled with a name, some of which were nearly identical. There were so many sisters that their parents had given many of them the same first names, with numbers as middle names. Which meant Amphitrite had a little sister named Amphitrite Two. And Thetis had two sisters named after her, a Two *and* a Three. It could get confusing.

Not looking where she was going, Amphitrite almost bumped into her dad.

"Heard you went looking for Halia this morning. She didn't venture onto land, did she?" he demanded in greeting. He had a beard and a long serpentine merman tail, and he wore a netted cloak that was covered with small treasures he'd collected from the sea. Some were gold doubloons or bits of coral or shell in interesting shapes. Others were fishing lures he'd stolen right off the lines trailing from fishing boats!

"Huh?" Amphitrite faced her dad. "Halia knows she would need your permission for that," she replied quickly. She hadn't exactly fibbed, but she crossed her fingers behind her back as she treaded water with slow swishes of her tail.

Her little sisters didn't always obey rules. She and Thetis hadn't either, when they were younger. Their dad's rules were pretty strict. Mostly they were meant to keep everyone safe. Still, the lure of the land was strong for the more adventurous merpeople, despite the dangers. Amphitrite herself felt it more and more each day. Mostly, she kept her yearnings a secret. Until her slip with Thetis that morning, that is.

"Your mom and I rely on you and Thetis to keep an eye on things—especially sisters and seals—

around here," her dad went on. "We're busy. We need to know we can count on you."

Amphitrite nodded. "I know. We'll try to do better." She and Thetis had seal-herding class twice a week, and she knew her dad expected them to take charge of his seals someday. *Borring!* Although Thetis was wild about seal herding, Amphitrite definitely was not. However, her dad was pretty much the boss in this part of the sea, and few dared defy his wishes. Including her! Besides, she loved her family and wanted her dad to be proud of her. She tried so hard to like seal herding and to fit in around here. But wouldn't everyone be surprised to know how she really felt!

"Hi, Dad," said Thetis, swimming up to join them. Her pet dragonfish was cowering inside her net schoolbag and darting worried glances around like he expected a bigger fish to attack at any minute.

Pets were allowed in class at MUMS. Even scaredy-fish, always-jabbering ones like Thetis's Dragon.

Their dad gave Thetis an approving smile. As usual, she was spared the lecture that Amphitrite had just been given. Which wasn't really fair, since both sisters were responsible for looking after the younger ones. But Thetis was given a pass. She was pretty much the star of the family, excelling at everything. It was kind of hard to live up to her example at times!

"Well, you two had better be off," said their dad. "You don't want to be late for class." Both girls gave him a quick hug. As they started off, he added, "Fingers crossed that we get an invitation to the Temple Games soon. It would be nice for the Undersea to be represented!" Smiling at the thought, he punched a fist in the water. The force sent a huge underwater current that would probably rock a few hapless ships when it eventually reached the surface of the Aegean Sea.

"Yeah! Bye, Dad," both girls chimed. Then they whooshed off.

In minutes, they reached the school's entrance, which was formed by the prow of an ancient sunken pirate ship. The door in the schoolship was really just a large hole that had probably been caused when it had wrecked on some sunning rocks during a storm long ago. High above the entrance on the front tip of the ship there was a beautiful painted lady carved from wood. Sometimes before tests, the girls knocked on her on their way inside, hoping she'd bring them good luck.

The two mermaid sisters had the same first period shifting class. It wasn't Amphitrite's favorite class by a long shot, though it might have been if she'd ever experienced any success at it. But unlike most other students, she could only go through the motions and learn the rules, not actually shape-shift.

The amazing Thetis had learned to switch from tail to legs way back when they were toddlers. By now, she could transform into many other things. On land, she could become a burning flame or even take the shape of a lion. Undersea, she could become a serpent to scare other creatures away, or a seahorse to hide from danger.

Today Thetis was coaxing Amphitrite to attempt a simple form and function shift. The idea was to magically transform herself into a patch of sunlight through willpower. A handy blending-in skill if you were ever caught on land by mortals or undersea by predators.

"Imagine you are a tasty plankton roll baking on a sunning rock," suggested Thetis, causing them both to giggle. "You're getting warm . . . then hot . . . then hotter . . . then sizzling," she went on.

Dutifully, Amphitrite thought warm thoughts and chanted:

> *"Golden scales to golden light.*
>
> *Change girl to sun, shining bright!"*

"Anything?" Thetis asked, studying her sister's face hopefully.

"Um, maybe a little tingle in the tip of my left tailfin? I'm not sure," Amphitrite replied, though she was pretty sure that was just wishful thinking. Despite her frustration, she remained ever hopeful. She could hardly wait till her very first shift happened. *If* it happened. Exchanging her tail for legs and walking on land would be a dream come true! Even if it only lasted a few minutes.

After shifting came sunning and singing class with

Ms. Siren. Usually S and S was held in the MUMS gym, but today the class was going on a field trip to poke around an old shipwreck in hopes of finding sheet music on board. If they found some, they could learn some new sailor songs to sing. Amphitrite hoped she might also stumble across a new adventure-story scrollbook she could read after she finished the one in her bag. Any scrolls they found would be treated with magic to keep them from rotting underwater.

Once aboard the sunken ship, she and Thetis began searching through a cupboard behind a water-logged piano. Suddenly they heard a mermaid near them give a yelp of surprise. They both looked over in time to see that a bubble as big as her head had bumped up against the girl.

"Jumping jellyfish! Sneak up on a merperson,

why don't you?" the girl scolded the bubble as it bounced off her and bobbled around underwater.

"A giant bubble! Run away!" wailed Thetis's pet dragonfish. He had detached himself from her bag so that he could explore freely, but now he dashed over and clung to it again.

"Don't tell me you're scared of a bubble," Amphitrite teased Dragon.

"Only of ones bigger than me," he replied in his small voice.

As the bubble bounced up to the ceiling of the wreck to bump another student, both sisters gazed up at it. "It's not one big bubble. It's four small bubbles stuck together, see?" Thetis said, pointing.

Amphitrite squinted at the quadbubble. "Yeah, and I see letters and words inside it!"

"Think it's a message? I wonder who sent it?" said Thetis, squinting too.

Dragon peeked out. "Probably a dark force of evil," he said shakily.

Amphitrite grinned. "Let's pop it and see." She curled her tail, preparing to push off toward the four-celled bubble that was bobbling around overhead. But just then it unstuck itself and floated away. Joined by other students who had just noticed the strange bubble too, Amphitrite chased after it. Dragon groaned and muttered something about bubble rhyming with trouble, but no one listened.

"Who got the *bubble-graaam*?" Ms. Siren sang out as it floated past her. She had an amazing voice and could sing all kinds of songs, from folk to pop rock to classical, and everything in between. But her favorites were sea shanties.

Amphitrite swished her head toward the teacher. *Bubble-gram? So that bubble really must contain a message of some kind!*

"You can all stop chasing it," the teacher sang out. "It will only pop when it bumps whoever its message is meant for." She clapped her hands together. "Everybody back to work. Ignore the bubble unless it happens to break for *yooou!*"

Reluctantly, everyone went back to searching the ship. And the bubble-gram continued its journey, bumping students at random, yet never popping. Finally, it headed back toward Amphitrite and Thetis.

"Yikes! It'll flatten me like a sand dollar!" Dragon zoomed away to hide behind an old wooden desk covered with barnacles.

The bubble-gram bumped Amphitrite's arm. To her surprise, one of its bubbles broke. *Pop!*

Stunned, she silently watched as letters and squiggles spilled from the bubble to form a map in the sand on the floor of the shipwreck. Before she had time to study the map, however, another of the bubbles burst. *"Be at the Delphi temple tomorrow morning,"* a tiny voice called out.

"Me? Why?" Amphitrite asked, still not understanding.

"Shh—there's more," said Thetis, who had seen what was happening and swum up beside her. So far they were the only ones to have noticed that the four-part bubble had begun to burst.

A third bubble burst. *"You are hereby invited to participate in the Temple Games."*

Amphitrite and Thetis looked at each other, their eyes wide. "Temple Games?" Amphitrite repeated in astonishment. Instant, impossible hope rose up in her.

"You've been invited to the Temple Games!" said Thetis, hugging her.

Then the last bubble burst: *"This message is for Thetis Of-the-Sea,"* it chirped. Of-the-Sea was their last name, given that their dad's official name was Old Man Of-the-Sea.

"Thetis?" Amphitrite echoed dully. Looked like the bubble-gram had mistaken her for her twin, even though they looked nothing alike. Now this bad-news bubble had just burst *her* bubble!

Frowning, Thetis swam down to study the map. Amphitrite did too. It appeared to show the way to the Temple at Delphi in Greece. They'd studied temples in land geology class, so Amphitrite knew that they were fancy buildings dedicated to Mount Olympus immortals.

"The bubbles must have burst in backward order,"

Thetis murmured. "So we heard the last part of the message first and the first part of it last."

"Yeah, I kind of figured that out already," Amphitrite replied. Despite her disappointment, she didn't want to spoil Thetis's happiness at being chosen. So she smiled and wrapped an arm around her sister's shoulders. "Congratulations on your invitation!" she said, making her voice sound perky.

"Not so fast!" Thetis shot a secretive look over at the other students and Ms. Siren. They were all excitedly exclaiming over a trunk full of sea shanty music someone had discovered on the opposite side of the ship. "No one heard that message but us."

"So?"

"So you should be the one to go to the games."

Amphitrite drew her head back in surprise. "What? But you were invited, not me."

"I don't really want to go, though. I'd rather stay here," said Thetis. "You're the one who wants to travel and see the landworld. Well, here's your chance. For the whole week of the games!"

"But . . ." Amphitrite quickly sorted through the zillion reasons why what her sister was suggesting was impossible. Settling on one, she replied, "But I can't shift."

Thetis rolled her eyes, grinning. "So? Maybe whoever sent the invitation doesn't even care whether I can shape-shift. Just go. Pretend you're me. Tell everyone your name is Thetis. Who's going to know?"

"That would be . . . ," Amphitrite began, shaking her head. But before she could say, "cheating," Thetis interrupted.

"Perfect. That's what it would be."

Amphitrite just stared at her sister, hardly able to

67

believe that she was willing to give up such an amazing opportunity. Then she shook her head again, her hair swirling in the water this way and that. "No, it's too big a sacrifice. You should go. You're the one they want. And you could win, too. But me? I wouldn't have a chance. I'd let down everyone in the mer community."

"I'm telling you, I don't want to go!" Thetis insisted. "You'll be doing me a huge favor. Honest. Plus, you're wrong about your chances."

Hope rose in Amphitrite once again. This was her opportunity to have a real adventure, not just read about them. And Thetis *wanted* her to go. "Um, well, I . . . are you sure?"

Suddenly, something large came barreling through Undersea toward the shipwreck. "Alert! Hide, students!" Ms. Siren shouted in alarm, probably fearing it might be a shark or a dangerous octopus. However, it was zipping through the water much too fast to be either. Before anyone could make a move, it arrived. Parking itself in the middle of the wreck, the large thing gazed around at the students, eyeing them uncertainly.

"It's a hippocampus!" someone shouted. Sure enough, the creature had the head of a horse, two front hooves, and a flowing mane. But its back half ended in a serpentine fish tail covered with green scales.

"Transportation to the Temple at Delphi!" it whinnied, in explanation for its presence.

"Over here!" called Thetis. Quickly she explained to everyone, including Ms. Siren, that Amphitrite had been invited to the games. Amongst their cheers, Amphitrite found herself practically dragged over to the hippocampus.

"Hop on," Thetis urged. When Amphitrite still hesitated, her twin and some of their friends gave her a boost. Two seconds later, she found herself sitting sidesaddle on the hippocampus's back, with her tail draped over to one side.

The whole class followed Amphitrite and the hippocampus up to the surface of the sea. Once she and her magical mount broke through the water, they all said the chant that would allow a mermaid's tail to shift to legs.

"Legs from tail. Feet from fin.

Sea to Land. Change . . . begin!"

Nothing happened, of course. *How embarrassing!* It seemed that in their excitement they'd all forgotten she couldn't shape-shift. An uncomfortable silence fell as they remembered.

But then all of a sudden, Amphitrite's tail did a

weird wobbly shiver. She straightened in her seat, her fingers tightening in the hippocampus's mane. "Something's changing," she trilled. "I think I'm getting . . . legs?"

Treading water nearby, Thetis gasped and clapped her hands, her ponytail bobbing in her excitement. "You're shifting, aren't you? For the very first time, you're shifting! It's a sign!"

"A sign? What kind of sign?"

Thetis leaned closer and looked her in the eyes. "That we're doing the right thing," she whispered. With that, she gave the hippocampus a push and backed away.

And before she could say "hold your seahorses!" Amphitrite was off to the games, riding across the Aegean Sea! In aquatic creatures class she'd learned that seahorses grew up to be hippocampi like her mount. Although they were fish, seahorses were not great swimmers. They beat their fins quickly (about fifty times a second), but nevertheless couldn't travel very fast. In fact, they usually held on to the same coral or seaweed for days before moving on.

This hippocampus, however, raced like the wind, plowing westward across the water's surface. Eventually, Amphitrite spotted inlets ahead where colorful fishing boats were docked. Would her mount gallop on its front legs once they reach shore? No! As they approached land, the hippocampus magically sprouted wings! It flew her over a vast island, then over a gulf where seagulls kept pace with them for a while. She'd never seen the seas from so high overhead. How bright they were, and how blue!

Next they flew above villages with white columned buildings and fountained courtyards. Low stone walls crisscrossed the countryside beyond, turning it into a patchwork quilt of greens and browns. There were forests and hills, and even a volcano. Things she'd only read about till now. She'd studied enough maps in land geology class to know they were soaring over mainland Greece, heading for the city of Delphi. And surely her dreams of traveling were only just beginning, for the Temple Games would likely take her many other places as well!

When day turned to night, Amphitrite slept with her arms wrapped around the neck of her mount, finally waking at dawn. The farther they flew and the more sights she saw, the more excited she became, and the more certain that she was *meant* to take Thetis's place at the games.

After all, she'd shifted! Looking down, she reassured herself it was still true. That the cute golden

73

chiton she was now wearing hadn't changed back into a tail. That she had legs! Thetis was right. It *had* to be a sign that she was doing the right thing.

She tugged her skirt so she could switch to riding astride, her thoughts moving as fast as her mount. In Delphi she could make a fresh start, since no one knew her there. She'd call herself Thetis and become the new, adventurous, amazing, *shape-shifting* girl she'd always wanted to be!

Finally, the winged hippocampus landed at the bottom of a long path. There was a sign posted to one side of the path that read: *Sacred Way to the Delphi Temple*. Looking up ahead, she could see that the path wound up a hill. At the top, a crowd of kids about her age had gathered around some white buildings. One of them had to be the temple. And the kids must be the other contestants in the games, she thought excitedly.

"Thanks for the ride," she told the hippocampus. Then she hopped off it. And promptly crumpled to the ground. In all her dreams of having legs and walking on land, she'd never imagined *this* happening!

Oh, dribbles! As Amphitrite picked herself up and started uphill, she hoped no one had witnessed her tumble. She'd always imagined herself moving across land effortlessly, like she'd seen her sisters and mortals onshore do. The truth of the matter was that walking was hard! You had to think about where to place your every step or you'd topple over.

Out of the sea, her balance was totally out of whack. But maybe her walking ability would improve with practice. Putting one unsteady bare foot in front of the other, she continued up the path.

Near the top, she met a goddessgirl with long

glossy red hair. There were daisies tucked in it here and there.

"Hi. I'm Persephone, the goddess of growing things," she told Amphitrite. "Aphrodite and I are helping to register newly arrived team members." She looked down at the clipboard she was holding. "And you are?"

"I'm Amphit—" *Oops!* Amphitrite caught herself just in time. "Sorry, I mean, um . . . I'm Thetis. Thetis Of-the-Sea."

Persephone put a little check mark on her clipboard, and then waved her onward to the temple. "Welcome to the Temple Games, Thetis!"

4

The Gathering

Poseidon

IT WAS TUESDAY MORNING, AND ALL THE TEMPLE Games teams were gathering at Delphi for final instructions. Poseidon, along with his teammates Hades, Pandora, and Delphinius, had just arrived, when a girl called out to him. "Poseidon?"

He turned toward her, raising his eyebrows in question. She was standing a few feet away, looking at him uncertainly. Her eyes dropped to his chest, studying the ribbons and pins he'd fastened to his tunic—favors sent to him by mortals for luck—then she looked back at his face.

Shoving her long turquoise hair behind her ears with both hands, she cleared her throat. "Hi," she said. Then, with her hands clenched against the sides of her gold scalloped chiton, she took a wobbly step forward. Now that she was a little closer, he noticed that her eyes were almost the same turquoise color as his own. And she was barefoot.

"I'm Amph—, um, I mean, I'm *Thetis*. Persephone told me I'm on your team," she announced.

"Yeah, that's right," Poseidon replied.

Before he could go on, a rainbow shot across the sky. His eyes lifted to see another team captain—the goddessgirl Iris—come sliding down it to land in the temple courtyard. She and her MOA teammates, Antheia (goddess of flowered wreaths) and Hephaestus (god-boy of blacksmithing) arrived behind her via the colorful arc too. As the goddessgirl of rainbows, Iris could magically create them in all sorts of amazing shapes and sizes, and also use them as travel devices.

"So . . . um . . . what happens next?" the turquoise-haired Thetis asked, drawing Poseidon's attention again. When he turned his gaze back to her, she giggled a little, making a bubbly sound.

He frowned. "Something funny?" he asked, even though he'd already guessed she was just nervous.

"No," she replied, but a cloudy look came into her face.

Poseidon knew he was being kind of mean to her, but he was mega stressed out. His team would be facing stiff competition. And although he'd known it was unlikely, he'd been kind of hoping she wouldn't show. Then he could have chosen an alternate.

Finally, he said to her, "Once the teams are all here, we'll be given a clue as to the location of our first challenge in the games."

"Fizzy!" Thetis exclaimed, brightening. "I can hardly wait to get started!"

Poseidon raised his eyebrows again. He hadn't forgotten what that Oracle-O fortune cookie had predicted yesterday at dinner. That this Thetis girl might outshine him. *Humph!* She'd better not try. *He* was going to be the victor in these games. *Her* role, like that of the other members of his team, was to support him. To make sure he earned himself a fabulous temple to rival those his friends already had. Because that was the grand prize that would go to the captain of whichever team won.

Seeing Pandora nearby, he called her over. "Pandora? This is Thetis, a Nereid from the Aegean Sea," he told her. "She's on our team. Introduce her to the guys, will you? Then show her where the winged sandals are. We might need to do some flying soon."

At this, Thetis put one foot atop the other, like she wanted to hide her bare feet. When she almost fell over, she quickly planted both feet firmly on the ground again.

"Aye-aye, Captain?" said Pandora, giving him a mock salute in answer to his order. That girl could make anything into a question, but at least she seemed to understand clearly that *he* was in charge of their team.

Pandora smiled at Thetis. "So you're a mergirl? How cool is that?" Before the girl could reply, Pandora added, "I'm so excited about the games, aren't you? Hey, want to meet Delphinius and Hades?"

Poseidon couldn't help grinning. With her endless questions, Pandora would help keep Thetis out of his hair. While his team members got acquainted, he carefully noted who was on the other teams as they landed and assembled.

Ares' team arrived by chariot. His two MOA members were the squinty-eyed Makhai and a burly godboy named Kydoimos, both of whom had been known to cheat if there was anything to be gained by it. It was a mystery why Zeus had chosen them for this competition. They were Ares' friends, of course. Also, rumor had it they'd been trying to mend their ways lately, so maybe putting them in the games was intended to be some kind of encouragement or reward.

Ares' two non-MOA members included an exotic goddessgirl with kohl-lined eyes whose name he couldn't quite recall. And his sister Eris, too—a surprising choice, since Ares didn't get along with her. However, come to think of it, his sister might actually be a *smart* choice. Since she was the goddess of discord, she could help him by starting arguments among the other teams.

"We'll have to be on guard against Ares' sister causing trouble among us," he noted in a murmur to himself. Feeling the need for some kind of action, he pulled out a pumice stone and began using it to sharpen the prongs of his trident. It was a mindless, soothing task that would still allow him to concentrate on the other teams.

"Yeah. She's good at that," said Hades, overhearing. "Remember how she even had Athena and Aphrodite at each other's throats for a while after Ares' last birthday? And those two are usually like *that*." He held up a hand with his forefinger and middle finger tightly crossed.

Poseidon nodded. "True. I know I've seen his fourth before, but I can't remember her name."

Pandora looked over. "That's Isis, Aphrodite's goddess friend from Egypt, remember? She came to MOA during the girls' Olympics?"

"Oh yeah," said Poseidon, recognizing her now. As he watched, Aphrodite ran over and hugged the Egyptian girl. Both of them were astoundingly beautiful. They hadn't always been friends, though. There had been a contest between them a while back to decide which was the true goddess of love and beauty. Probably a good thing it had been declared a tie, or they might never have become what girls were always calling each other: BFFs, as in Best Friends Forever.

Hades looked around as if raring to get this contest started. "A beauty queen like Isis is an unexpected choice," he commented.

"Or maybe it's genius," said Poseidon.

"Why's that?" Thetis asked. Her feet were planted wide now, as if she was halfway through a jumping jack. Or bracing against a strong wind.

"I bet I know!" blurted Pandora. "Ares must think teams will be sent to an Egyptian temple at some point during the games? One where Isis's knowledge will be helpful?"

Poseidon stopped sharpening his trident and put a fingertip to his nose to indicate she'd hit it right on the nose. "Exactly my thought." He wished it had occurred to him to invite Isis first, though. Instead of Thetis. Winning the Temple Games would not only require skill and strength, but careful strategy as well. As the godboy of war, Ares had all three going for him.

"C'mon, want to go meet some of the others?" Pandora grabbed Thetis's hand and started across the temple courtyard, heading toward Athena's team.

Of all the teams, Poseidon figured Athena's would be hardest to beat. The brainiest goddessgirl at MOA, she'd always been his number one competition. It still rankled that her olive, which could be used for oil as well as food, had beat out his water park in an inventions contest when she'd first come to MOA. That had resulted in the Greeks naming their newest, biggest city after her instead of him. Athens instead of Poseidonville.

Since Heracles was on her team, they had brains and *brawn* going for them. Her other team members included the godboy Dionysus and goddessgirls named Panacea and Harmonia.

Poseidon frowned as he noticed something. Halfway across the courtyard, his newest team member was limping. "Thetis, wait up!" he called to her. But Pandora had her firmly by the hand and they kept going. "Thetis!" he called again. Tucking his pumice stone back in the pocket of his tunic, he hurried after them. When he finally caught up, both girls paused.

"Didn't you hear me call your name?" he asked Thetis.

She let go of Pandora's hand. "Um, sorry, no," she said. Her eyes shifted away, then back to him, like she had some secret. She was probably just nervous, he reminded himself.

He gestured toward her legs. "You're limping."

"Oh? Are you hurt?" Pandora asked her worriedly.

"I'm fine," Thetis said quickly. "Just getting my land legs, that's all. You know how it is. I'm a mermaid. Always swimming. Takes a while to adjust to walking." She laughed her bubbly laugh again.

"If you say so," Poseidon said with a scowl. He couldn't have her holding back the team by being unable to keep up. That would be as bad as her trying to take over and *outshine* him as leader!

Pandora tugged at Thetis's arm. "C'mon, then. Ready to go meet everyone else?"

"Sure," said Thetis. Before she was towed away, she surprised him with a quick grin that sent sparkles into her eyes. "Guess we'll see you later, Captain," she told him.

He was still staring after Thetis when Hades and Delphinius came over to him. "Apollo just got here," Hades announced, pointing across the courtyard.

"He brought his bow and golden arrows," Delphinius observed. Then he added in a confident tone, "But even with magic arrows, he won't be a threat to our team."

That was one of the great things Poseidon remembered about his loyal childhood friend. Delphinius was always ready with an encouraging word and had his back when things got tough.

His comments started a discussion among the three boys about the perceived strengths and weaknesses of Apollo's team members. An excellent archer himself, Apollo had chosen two others skilled in the sport—the godboy Eros and a mortal named Actaeon (who was also his sister's crush). Rounding out his team was a half-boy, half-horse MOA student named Centaur and a Titan named Epimetheus (who was Pandora's crush).

"I'm surprised Apollo didn't invite Cassandra," Poseidon noted. "With their combined gifts of prophecy, they'd have a real edge at winning the games." Plus, everyone knew she was Apollo's crush.

"Didn't you read the contest rules Ms. Hydra drew up?" a girl's voice interrupted. Pheme had flitted over, her wings so soundless no one had noticed her approach. "They specifically say that magical prophecy is forbidden. So Apollo can't use his gift to learn what's coming up, and he wasn't allowed to invite Cassandra." As usual, her words puffed from her lips, written in cloud letters that hung over their heads for anyone to read.

"Uh, thanks," said Poseidon. "Well, see you." He nudged Delphinius with an elbow and shot Hades a look that said they'd better move along. They didn't need Pheme broadcasting their speculations about the other teams.

Just then, strong winds suddenly swept the temple

courtyard. Hearing shrieks of laughter, Poseidon looked over to see a group of girls that included Persephone, Aphrodite, Panacea, Harmonia, Medusa, Pandora, and Thetis. They were all trying to smooth their hair (or snakes, in Medusa's case) and hold onto their skirts as the wind kept gusting. Thetis was wearing winged sandals now, he noticed.

"What in the Underworld? Where's that wind coming from?" asked Hades, looking around in surprise.

"From Iris's team. Her last two members just arrived," said Delphinius, hooking a thumb in the newcomers' direction. Poseidon glanced over at them as he absently finger-combed his windblown blond hair back into its usual perfect style. Iris had apparently invited Zephyr and Boreas, two god-boy winds, to be on her team. Zephyr controlled the warm west wind of spring, and his brother, the

91

white-haired Boreas, controlled the cold winter wind.

A few minutes later, Poseidon, Hades, and Delphinius met up with Pandora and Thetis again. "Learn anything about our enemies' strategies?" Poseidon asked the two girls.

"Enemies? I hope you're only joking," said Pandora.

"Sure he is. Right?" Thetis asked him, shooting him an uncertain look.

"It's us against them. We are in this to win this," Poseidon said, punching a fist sideways in an effort to get them pumped up and seeing things his way.

"Uh . . . right, Captain," Hades agreed.

Delphinius nodded enthusiastically. "You bet!"

"So, no, we are not joking," said Poseidon, eyeing the two girls sternly. "Until this contest is over, our only friends are the ones on this team or those who can help us move forward in the games." He thought he saw Pandora elbow Thetis and roll her eyes, but wasn't sure. With an inward sigh, he hoped these girls would take this contest seriously.

"Attention, everyone! Welcome to the official opening of the Temple Games!" Persephone and Aphrodite suddenly called out from the top of the temple's front steps. Zeus had apparently enlisted them to give instructions, since they weren't on any of the teams themselves.

"First off, any new team members, listen up," said Persephone, gazing out over the crowd. "You'll each need to grab one of these white scrolls on your way into the temple." She picked up a small scroll from an urn full of some like the ones all MOA students had gotten from Hermes yesterday, and waggled it high in her fingers to show everyone.

"They state the rules, but are also magical," Aphrodite

explained. "Which means all of your scrolls can receive information. They can't send it, however. Pheme has got the only scroll with two-way communication. So she's the only student who can send messages to us or Principal Zeus. For now, though, all you need to know is that you'll be visiting six other temples after this one."

"And at each of those other temples you'll be given a challenge," continued Persephone. "A task you'll have to perform successfully in order to move on. The longer it takes you, the bigger the lead that other, faster teams will gain."

Aphrodite nodded, adding, "No one will be eliminated here at Delphi. But one team will be knocked out at each temple you visit after this one. Next five temples, five teams out. The games will end at the sixth temple, where the last two of our seven teams will compete in a final challenge that will result in one victor."

"Us!" shouted Ares, grinning.

"No, us!" Artemis countered, a wide smile on her face.

"You wish! Victory!" yelled Poseidon, raising his trident high. He sure hoped one or more of the temple challenges would involve water and swimming since that's where his team would have the greatest advantage.

"Dream on!" called Athena, laughing. More cries of good-natured joking about who would win circulated.

Persephone and Aphrodite called for everyone's attention again, then went on for a while longer about the minor prizes and ribbons that all participants would receive at the end of the games. However, Poseidon hadn't been joking before about his determination to win. All he was really interested in was prize numero uno. The grand prize. His very own temple.

Eventually, he tuned back in to see Aphrodite motioning behind her to the temple building. It had six tall stone columns across the front. The wide triangular pediment that rested atop them was made of marble and carved with sculptures of gods and goddesses. "When you go inside, the Oracle of Delphi herself will provide an important clue," she was saying. "You'll need to decipher that clue to figure out where to travel next to receive your first challenge in the games."

Creak! The temple doors swung open, pulled from the inside by guards. Teams began to push forward in their hurry to get started.

"Good luck, everyone! Let the games begin!" Persephone and Aphrodite called out together in bright voices. Then the two goddessgirls moved to stand on either side of the temple entrance to avoid getting run over as everyone stampeded past.

Once inside the temple, Poseidon gazed around in wonder. Everywhere he looked he saw baskets and urns piled high with all kinds of gifts brought by Apollo's worshippers. Apollo was the star here because the Temple of Delphi was *his* temple. Earth mortals had offered him everything from beaded bracelets and woven blankets to gold vases! There were plenty of statues around the temple too, especially of Zeus and Apollo.

"Isn't this cool?" Pandora said from behind him.

"I know! It's fizztastic! I can't believe I'm here," Thetis replied. She sounded super excited and awed.

This was exactly the kind of temple Poseidon longed to have. But one that was dedicated to him, of course. A place that would wow mortals and show them how important and mega-amazing he was.

Naturally his temple would have a tremendous fountain at its center. With a statue of him in the middle riding a team of two, no, *three* hippocampi. As water looped and sprayed rhythmically around him, his trident would be raised high in battle. *Awesome!* Having his own temple would officially make him a top-tier godboy like Apollo and several of his other friends at MOA who already had their own temples.

The walls of the other rooms they passed through after leaving the main room were covered with more paintings and carvings of Apollo doing cool stuff. There was one of him shooting his bow and arrow at monsters and another of him playing his lyre. Poseidon even noticed a small statue of himself, since he was among Apollo's friends at Mount

Olympus Academy. That was nice, but it wasn't nearly enough.

When the teams finally reached the inner sanctuary at the back of the temple, they found themselves in a small dim room. All thirty-five participants crowded in and formed a circle around the Oracle. She was seated in the center of the room on a high golden stool and was wearing an enormous red cloak. Its hood threw deep shadows over her face.

Looking around the circle, Poseidon saw Apollo, Ares, Artemis, Athena, Iris, and Medusa with their teams. And Pheme. The small wings at her back were gently fluttering, carrying her around the room as she wrote rapidly on the scroll-gadget Zeus had given her. She was probably describing everything inside the temple, telling the rest of the world every detail of what happened here.

Medusa's two assigned MOA members were her immortal sisters, Stheno and Euryale. She'd also apparently chosen two Chinese goddessgirls that he didn't know. He overheard her call them Wen Chi and Mazu. They were the only all-girl team.

Artemis was carrying her bow and a quiver of her magic silver arrows, and was flanked by her MOA team members, Aglaia and a lizard-tailed boy named Ascalabus. She'd also invited two strong-looking non-MOA girls. One of them was wearing dozens of silver bracelets that jangled on her arms whenever she moved.

Poseidon pointed the girls out to Apollo, who happened to be standing next to him. "Amazons?" he whispered.

"Yeah," Apollo whispered back. "Penthesilea and Hippolyta. Both archers."

Just then, a priest dressed in a long white robe appeared. Stepping to one side of the Oracle, he welcomed everyone in a quiet voice. "You've come at a very special time. One of only nine days a year during which Oracle Pythia may be visited. Please be patient. Soon she will receive a message from the mysterious depths of the earth. You'll know this is happening when steam rises through the omphalos."

"The ompha-what?" joked Ares. The priest sent him a sour look. Ares took the hint and clammed up.

"The omphalos," the priest went on. "It is through this sacred stone that the Oracle receives information and prophecies." He pointed at an egg-shaped stone about three feet tall that sat balanced on one end upon a little table next to the Oracle. It was carved with a pattern of crisscross lines that resembled a fishing net, and had a hole about six inches in diameter in its top.

"Once Oracle Pythia divines the location of the first temple you are to visit, she will offer you a clue to its name. No prize will be awarded to any team for guessing the name. However, the sooner you figure it out, the better. The first teams to arrive at the temple will have the best chance at winning the first challenge."

At this, a silent tension filled the room, all eyes glued to the Oracle now. Yet still she sat motionless beside the egg on her high golden stool, her long cloak draped around her. Below her stool, Poseidon noticed a deep crack in the dirt floor, which also ran beneath the stone egg's table and then disappeared into the shadows at the back of the room.

Finally, the Oracle began to speak in a low croon.

"Long ago, the mighty Zeus called upon two eagles, each perched at opposite ends of our flat earth. He bade them to rise into the sky and fly toward one another at the same swift speed." Her arm swung out and she gestured dramatically at the stone egg. "It is here in this very spot that the noble birds met. Together, they landed upon this omphalos. And so it was that Zeus declared it to be the very center of the earth!"

Solemnly, she turned to face the stone egg. "Speak to me. Speak to me, sacred omphalos!" she coaxed, her voice rising with every word.

Everyone leaned in to listen to whatever the stone egg might say.

5

Being Thetis

Amphitrite

AMPHITRITE STOOD IN THE TEMPLE SANCTU-ary with her team, feeling totally thrilled. So far her deception seemed to be working. No one suspected she wasn't her sister Thetis. And the fun was just beginning.

She could hardly believe she was here in this amazing temple. *Standing! On legs!* But her head was still *swimming* with all the sights she'd seen on her travels so far. And she'd met real gods and goddesses that she and her sisters had only read about in *Teen Scrollazine*! Now she was gathered among them waiting for this sacred object—the omphalos—to speak to a famous oracle. It was all just so epic!

Slowly Oracle Pythia lifted her arms. Her hood fell back slightly, revealing a hint of her face with its dark eyes, straight nose, and thin lips.

Pssst! As if on cue, a great burst of steam hissed from the crack in the earthen floor and rose to fill the egg-shaped stone. The stone must be hollow, Amphitrite realized. Because the steam then funneled through it and out the opening at its top, mounting ever higher until it enveloped the Oracle. More steam followed in a loud gush, swirling and whooshing from the floor, through the egg, and then out into the room.

Through the foggy steam, Amphitrite could just make out that the Oracle had closed her eyes and begun to sway from side to side on her stool. Seeming unaware of her audience, she hummed tunelessly. Her outstretched arms moved gracefully, like those of a mystical dancer, her hands causing the steam to leap and curl. For long moments, the thirty-five students waited, entranced. At last, she spoke the clue that would hint at where temple they should all visit next. It was short:

"All . . .

With a single eye,

it can cry,

but only when it rains."

Finished, Pythia straightened her arms, folded both hands in her lap, and went silent again. The priest made sweeping motions with his arms to dismiss all thirty-five students. As they shuffled from the room, Amphitrite wished she knew what the Oracle's clue meant. Glancing at the others' faces, she could tell they were pretty puzzled too.

Pheme flitted among them, listening in as each team whispered among themselves. All were trying to figure out the answer to the riddle the Oracle had posed, so they'd know which temple to visit next and could beat the other teams to it.

Because Amphitrite's team had been at the far side of the sanctuary, they were last to file out. "Thoughts?" Poseidon asked her, Pandora, Hades, and Delphinius as they started back through the temple. At the same time, he unrolled his purple team leader scroll and scanned it for information that might help to decode the clue. But it seemed he saw at once that there was nothing in the scroll to help them. "So what's our destination?" he prompted his team as he let the scroll snap shut and stuffed it back in his pocket. "Where do we go to get our first challenge in the games?"

"Is it something to do with Mr. Cyclops?" Pandora suggested as they retraced their steps past walls lined with statues and art treasures.

Amphitrite had read about him in *Teen Scrollazine*. MOA's famed hero-ology teacher had a single big eye in the middle of his forehead.

Delphinius cocked his head, thinking. "He does have only one eye, but has anyone ever seen him cry when it rains?"

"I've never seen him cry at all," said Poseidon.

"Me neither," said Hades.

Pandora nodded her agreement. "Not a single tear, rain or shine."

"Besides that, there's no temple dedicated to him that I've ever heard of," said Delphinius. "So he can't be the answer."

"If we're lucky, the Oracle's clue might mislead some teams and send them to Sicily—that island off the coast of Italy—though," offered Hades. "That's where Mr. Cyclops is from."

As they neared the temple exit, Amphitrite got an idea. She touched Pandora's arm to get her attention. "Hey, remember what Panacea told us when we met her and Harmonia earlier? She said that—"

Just then Amphitrite's legs began to tremble and wobble, like seaweed in a swift undersea current. She stumbled, lost her balance, and bumped into the wall behind her. *What was happening? Oh no! Was she shifting back into a mermaid?* But when she looked down, she saw that her legs were still firm and strong.

"What's going on?" said Delphinius, his eyes worried.

Pandora let go of a statue she'd been hugging for balance and shrugged uncertainly. "Earthquake?"

Amphitrite pushed off from the wall. "So you all felt that too?"

"Yeah! Are you kidding?" said Hades. "The whole building was shaking."

"Maybe we're under some kind of attack!" Poseidon exclaimed.

He and Hades moved to stand protectively at either side of their team, alert for danger. Their muscles were tense, their fists bunched. They looked ready to fend off any enemy who might suddenly appear.

None came, however. But the whole temple shuddered again, rocking back and forth so hard that everyone went flying. A fluted white column near Amphitrite cracked. Small bits of marble chipped from the ceiling and crumbled to the ground.

A cry came from over in the Oracle's sanctuary. Without thinking of the danger from falling chunks of stone, Amphitrite turned and rushed back through the temple. The rest of her team was close on her heels. They reached the small room that housed the omphalos just in time to hear a loud crunching sound. All five of them stopped short, eyes going wide at the sight that greeted them.

Boom! A giant fist, five times the size of any godboy's, punched its way up through the crack in the floor, ripping a huge hole in it. The fist's beefy fingers wrapped around the omphalos. Then the hand quickly withdrew back down into the hole it had made, taking the three-foot-tall stone egg with it.

Amphitrite gasped. Dashing over, she gazed down into the hole. The golden stool the Oracle had sat upon now lay on its side a short distance away.

"Not so close, Thetis," said Poseidon, taking her arm.

"Huh? Thetis? Where is she?" Startled, Amphitrite looked around for her sister. She was so stunned and shaken up that she'd momentarily forgotten everyone thought that *she* was Thetis.

"I mean, where is . . . the Oracle?" she quickly clarified. "And who took the omphalos!" She tried to look into the hole again, but Poseidon pulled her away from the crack. Just in time, too, because a large column tore itself loose from the wall and slammed down right where she'd been standing. *Bam!* Everyone drew back.

"What happened?" asked Athena, rushing into the small room. Her teammates, Heracles, Dionysus, Harmonia, and Panacea were right behind her. They all gaped at the new humongous hole in the floor.

Heracles gripped his massive club and held it at the ready as his eyes surveyed the sanctuary for possible danger.

Words burst from Amphitrite. "The omphalos is gone! A big fist punched up through the crack in the floor and stole it just now!"

Catching her eye, Poseidon frowned at her and shook his head. Did that mean he didn't like her sharing this information with Athena's team? Well, too bad! This was a crisis, unrelated to the competition. *Hmm.* Or *was* it related?

"*Ye gods!* My dad's sacred stone?" Athena rushed over to the table where the stone had so recently rested to look for clues regarding the thief.

"I don't get it," said Amphitrite. "Only the Oracle can make the omphalos tell prophecies. So why would anyone want to steal it?"

Poseidon swung around to Athena. "What do you know about that stone? Anything helpful?"

She shrugged. "Dad told me the two eagles he released to find the center of the world just found it sitting here when they met and settled on this spot. Oh, and he calls the omphalos the *bellybutton* of the world."

Despite the gravity of the situation, the students on both teams chuckled at this. Athena grinned and smoothed her long wavy brown hair to hang over one shoulder. "Dad does have a quirky sense of humor," she acknowledged. But then she grew serious again. "As for who the thief might be, I guess it's someone who wants to start trouble. I mean, my dad will be furious when he finds out it's gone."

"Finds out what's gone? What are you talking about? Where is the stone?" The Oracle had suddenly appeared from the shadows of the room, where she'd apparently been cowering. She tugged her hood back down, and Amphitrite could see that her dark eyes were terrified.

Righting her stool, she sat up on it and began to rock gently. While they tried to explain what had happened, she stared into the distance as if in a trance. "I see a great battle," she interrupted in an eerie voice. "This one will test the Olympians even more than the Titan war. A hundred fighters will soon come. Beware."

All ten students on Poseidon's and Athena's teams stared at her in horror. The long-ago war between the Titans and the Olympians had been terrible. Led by Zeus, however, the Olympians had prevailed in the end.

"Well, that doesn't sound good," said Hades, finally breaking the tension.

"I thought you couldn't make predictions without

the omphalos," Athena said to the Oracle.

"It is not a new prediction. I have seen it before," Pythia replied. Then she tugged her hood to shadow her face again. "That is all. You are right. My gift of prophecy is indeed gone."

"So you don't know who our opponents in this coming battle will be?" Poseidon pushed.

Her hooded head shook back and forth.

"I'm guessing that's a no," murmured Panacea, Athena's teammate.

"The Titans are our greatest enemies. You don't suppose that—" said Dionysus.

"No," interrupted Hades. "They didn't steal the omphalos. They're all safely locked up in Tartarus, remember?" He and Heracles were now kneeling with their eyes pressed along the crack in the floor, trying to see into the depths of the earth.

Heracles poked his club into the big hole the fist had made and moved it around, testing to see if he could locate anything or anyone. With a sigh, he stood, appearing to give up on finding any clues down there. "Yeah, that's what we thought about Typhon, though," he reminded Hades. "But he still somehow managed to escape."

Amphitrite shuddered. Everyone had heard about Typhon, even the merpeople. He was a monster made of whirling tornado-strength winds that had escaped from imprisonment in Tartarus not long ago. Tartarus was said to be the most awful place in the Underworld, where only the truly evil wound up. And he'd turned out to be evil, all right. He had ravaged many lands before attacking Mount Olympus Academy, too.

According to Pheme's column in *Teen Scrollazine*, the

goddessgirl Iris had bravely helped Zeus recapture the monster. Now Typhon was imprisoned in a new, secret location where he could never make trouble again.

"Hey, where is everyone?" asked Pandora, looking toward the sanctuary exit. "Why didn't the other teams come back?"

"They were farther ahead when we left, so maybe they didn't notice the shaking," suggested Delphinius.

"Or maybe they've already figured out the clue and gone ahead to the next temple," said Poseidon, sounding seriously worried. "C'mon. We should all get back to the games too."

"You want to continue with the Temple Games when we're under attack?" asked Amphitrite, astounded.

"Maybe we should discuss all this with the other teams," Harmonia said quickly. "Get their agreement in calling the games off for now."

"Well, I'm captain of my team, not you," Poseidon told her hotly. "And I say the games are still on for *my* team." With that, he, Hades, and Delphinius put their heads together to discuss the Oracle's original clue in low tones.

Amphitrite heard Athena speak to one of her teammates. "Panacea? Since Pheme can contact Principal Zeus with her scroll, would you go find her and ask her to message him about what's happened? As if to reassure everyone, she added, "He'll know what to do."

The very second Panacea departed, the Oracle piped up again, drawing everyone's attention. "Just remembered one last thing. Gaia is angry."

"Who's Gaia?" Pandora asked, cocking her head as she tried to place the somewhat familiar name.

"Goddess of the Earth," Hades replied in dark, ominous tones. "She's kind of moldy-smelling and is always hanging out around the River Styx that borders the Underworld. I'm pretty sure she encouraged Typhon to attack MOA."

Heracles frowned. "Why would she do that?"

"Because she's his *mom*," said Hades, which caused several students' eyes to widen in surprise. "And the Oracle's right about her being angry. Gaia is always ranting about how the Titans deserved to beat us in the Titan-Olympian war."

Quick footsteps sounded as three temple priests rushed in. Their faces paled at the damage they saw, and they scurried to the Oracle's side to make sure she was all right.

"Out, everyone. Shoo!" said the priest who had earlier welcomed the students to the temple. "Now!"

As Amphitrite hastened to leave along with everyone else, a tiny rock lodged in her sandal. Before she could bend to get it out, Athena fell into step with her.

"Poseidon's right, you know," Athena offered as they walked quickly. "Thanks to Zeus's magical scroll-gadgets, the whole world is watching. We don't want to panic anyone. So until we hear from him with other instructions, I agree we should get on with the competition."

Pandora caught up to walk with them on Amphitrite's other side. "You okay, Thetis? You're limping. Were you hurt in the quake back there?"

"No, I'm fine," said Amphitrite. "Just got something in my sandal is all." She paused, pressing one hand against the wall for balance as she pulled the little rock from her sandal.

When she straightened, she saw that Athena was staring hard at her. "You're Thetis? Of-the-Sea? Daughter of Nereus?" she asked.

"Mm-hm. That's me." The lie was coming more easily, but Amphitrite grew a little nervous at Athena's disbelieving expression. They hadn't actually been officially introduced earlier in the courtyard, but what if Athena knew her sister somehow? Or had seen a drawing of her somewhere? Had she guessed that Amphitrite was an imposter? *Shivering shrimps!* This must be how Pandora felt all the time, her brain whirling with questions.

"Sorry for staring," said Athena as they all hurried off again. "It's just that Aphrodite and I were assigned two kindergarten buddies named Thetis and Amphitrite from Mediterranean Undersea Kindergarten when their class visited MOA earlier this year. But they were just five years old, so . . ."

Relieved laughter bubbled up from Amphitrite's throat. "Those were—" she started to say.

But her words trailed off as they stepped out of the temple and into the sunlight and she suddenly realized why none of the other five teams had come back inside the sanctuary. Priests and guards were standing at the temple entrance. They had blocked the other teams from reentering, leaving them to hang around outside.

She, Athena, and Pandora were last out, and their teams were waiting at the bottom of the temple steps. Under Poseidon's frowning gaze, Harmonia was busy telling the other teams what had happened inside. He couldn't exactly stop her, though, since she wasn't on his team.

"I started to tell you that those were my little sisters you met," Amphitrite continued to Athena as the three girls rushed down the stairs. "There are fifty of us in my family, so our parents took the easy way out and gave some of us the same names. You met Amphitrite Two and Thetis Two. I'm Am—" Amphitrite barely caught herself in time. *Again*. She had to stop doing that! "I mean, I *am* Thetis One," she finished.

"That explains it, then," said Athena, smiling as they joined the others in the courtyard.

"My sisters talked about you all the time after their visit," Amphitrite added. "Still do. They adore you and Aphro—"

"Excuse me? Can we get back to important matters?" asked Poseidon, overhearing.

"Like the *games*?" Hades hinted pointedly.

Athena blinked at them, and then her expression turned determined as she refocused herself on the competition at hand. "Oh yeah. Right."

Amphitrite couldn't believe it. Didn't either of

these two team captains see that there were bigger things to worry about now than winning a game? Apparently not. As the others went on speaking, she opened her fist. She still had the forgotten pebble she'd pulled from her sandal, and now held it up to study it. With a fingertip, she brushed away the light layer of dust coating it. Underneath it was a lustrous, pale golden color, and perfectly round. It wasn't a rock at all. It was a pearl!

Before anyone could see, she quickly stuck it in her pocket (which was now in the skirt of her chiton), her mind racing. She hadn't come looking for pearls. But this one had found *her* by getting lodged in her sandal back in the sanctuary. It seemed more than a coincidence. What did it mean? Could it possibly have come from the legendary enchanted strand? Maybe there were more pearls in the sanctuary somewhere.

If so, that would explain why treasure-hunters who had searched for the legendary strand in the sea had never found it.

Just think! If she could locate the entire magical strand, there would be enough pearls for all forty-nine of her sisters. They could each make their own dearest wish come true. "And *my* wish would be to be able to live on land *or* sea!" she murmured under her breath.

She glanced up at the temple behind her. Unfortunately, the grouchy-looking guards at its front doors didn't look like they'd be up for letting her back in to look for more pearls. Not right now, anyway.

"Hello?" grumped Poseidon, drawing the attention of nearby students. "In case you haven't noticed, Artemis's team has left Delphi already. They must've figured out the riddle and gotten a head start on us."

Anxious murmurs arose among his team members. "We need to focus," Poseidon said, gesturing at them to huddle up. "Figure out our first destination. Until Zeus tells us otherwise, the games are on."

At that moment, Panacea finished speaking to Pheme as Athena had requested, and was passing by on her way to rejoin her team.

"Hey! I just remembered something I was going to say before. It's about the Oracle's clue," said Amphitrite, not bothering to keep her voice down. Stopping Panacea, she said, "Remember when we met in the courtyard, you told me how your whole name means a cure for all things? And that the 'pan' part of your name is the Greek word for 'all' like in the Oracle's clue?"

Pandora cocked her head curiously. "I wonder what my name means, then?"

Panacea opened her mouth as if planning to

answer, but Poseidon interrupted her. "Focus! This is no time for discussions of word origins," he said in exasperation. He looked at Amphitrite. "Why did you think the word 'pan' might be important?"

"Because there's a temple in Rome, Italy, called the *Pan*theon. The word means "*all* divine" because it's a temple dedicated to *all* Roman gods, not just one." Then suddenly she got excited, because she'd just remembered something else about that particular temple. "And it has a big open hole in its roof called an oculus!"

"Oculus. Like an *eye*!" said Athena, brightening. Amphitrite glanced around, realizing that all talk among the six teams that were still there had ceased, and she and Athena now had everyone's attention.

Heracles nodded. "An eye in the temple roof. So water could rain in during a storm."

"Which would make it look sort of like the temple was crying!" Amphitrite finished.

The other students stared at her, stunned. "How did you know—" Poseidon began.

She shrugged. "I read a lot, mostly about travel and adventure stuff. We have tons of sea scrolls scavenged from shipwrecks in our school library with all kinds of useful information about the world."

Pheme was writing on her scroll-gadget again. As everyone realized that Amphitrite had solved the Oracle's riddle, there was a sudden flurry of activity. Students began readying their various means of transportation to head for the city of Rome.

Teams took off, flying by chariot, cart, winged mount, winged sandal, or under the power of their own wings. Amphitrite watched Athena loosen the straps on her sandals to free the silver wings at her heels. Instantly the wings began to flutter and flap, causing the goddessgirl to rise and hover about six inches above the ground. Then she zoomed higher and away.

Amphitrite looked back at the temple door and sighed. The guards were still there. She'd have to wait till another time to get past them and search for more pearls.

"Let's go!" called Poseidon. He lifted off, as did the remaining teams.

Hurriedly, Amphitrite bent down and unleashed the wings on her sandals, just as she'd seen Athena do. But nothing happened. The sandals' wings remained stubbornly still. "C'mon, you dumb sandals. Let's go. What's wrong with you?" she scolded them.

Suddenly, a strong hand grabbed hers. "Whoa!"

she yelled. And just like that, she lifted off the ground and was pulled skyward!

"Only immortals can make the winged sandals work," Poseidon told her briskly. "So you'll need to keep hold of my hand."

Not needing to be told twice, especially with the ground zipping beneath her at a furious speed, Amphitrite held on tight.

6

First Challenge

Poseidon

POSEIDON SWOOPED DOWN AND GRABBED THETIS'S hand when he saw that she was unable to make her winged sandals fly. At his immortal touch, the wings on her sandals began to flutter, then flap.

"Whoa!" she said, sounding nervous. As they rose higher over Greece, her hand gripped his tightly, and she also clasped his arm with the fingers of her other hand. The wind whistled in his ears as he whisked them both away toward Rome.

After a few minutes, she calmed enough to smile up at him. "This is fun! And I'm not a bit scared."

Surprised by the happy gleam in her turquoise eyes, he grinned down at her. "Then why are you cutting off my circulation?" he couldn't resist asking. His eyes moved pointedly to her white-knuckled fingers digging into his arm. Laughing that bubbly laugh of hers, she loosened her grip a little, then let go. But her other hand still clasped his extra tight.

"No need to worry," he assured her. "As long as we're holding hands, your winged sandals will keep you aloft."

"Well, that's *handy*," she joked, giggling.

He smiled again, raising an eyebrow. She had a fun side that he was only just now beginning to appreciate. "I'm kind of surprised you can't fly on your own. Your dad's a god," he said.

"My mom's not a goddess though," she told him, her eyes on the scenery below. "She's half mortal, half mermaid."

"At least you've been able to swim and walk since you were a little kid, right?" he said. "That's two modes of transportation, anyway."

She shot him an uneasy glance, then looked away. "Uh, yeah."

What was that about? he wondered. But he often found girls hard to comprehend. And besides, he had other important stuff to think about right now. As they sped on, they saw other teams in the distance. All were moving in the same direction—northwestward toward Rome. However, none drew near enough to chat. Like him, they were focused on one goal—winning.

"Look—merpeople!" Thetis said a few minutes later. She was gazing raptly at the Ionian Sea below, which lay between Greece and Italy, north of the Mediterranean. Poseidon could see the flip of their tails when she pointed them out to him. There were pink-tailed ones, silver-tailed ones—tails in almost every color of the rainbow, in fact. Some of the mer-girls peeked out to wave, and Thetis waved back.

"Could we go down there?" she asked him. "I could really use a quick dip. I'm starting to feel like I'm drying out."

"I can fix that," said Poseidon. With his free hand, he twirled his trident above his head like a baton and said a quick magic spell:

"Water from the sea,

Rise up to me!

And fill prongs three."

Right away, the trident's three pronged tips began sprinkling Thetis with cool drops of saltwater that he'd somehow magically drawn up from the sea below. Startled by the sudden wet drops, she let go of his hand. "Help!" she cried out as she began to fall.

Like a shot, Poseidon raced down to catch her with his free arm. Once he had her in hand again, he threaded his fingers with hers to make it harder for their hands to slip apart. "Sorry," he said. "I guess I should've warned you before I did that. But those saltwater sprinkles will protect you for another twenty-four hours."

"Thanks," she said, still sounding breathless from her fall. "For the sprinkles *and* the rescue." Then her eyes flicked to something beyond him.

Following her gaze, Poseidon noticed that Ares' chariot, which had been far behind them a while ago, was now drawing near. Had he and his team seen what had just happened? Kind of embarrassing, because he and the guys prided themselves on not dropping those they winged sandal-transported.

"How did you do that trident sprinkle trick?" Thetis asked, pulling his attention back to her. "Is it something I could learn?" She stared at his trident eagerly.

He shook his head. "It's a spell I developed. Took me a year to get it right, and it only works for me, since I rule the seas."

"Oh." Her shoulders slumped. "I have a trident at home. It's the same turquoise color as my hair and all glittery. Not as big or powerful as yours, but I was kind of hoping you could teach me to do that same spell. Then my sisters and I would be free to travel on land as well as sea for as long as we liked without ever getting landsick."

She looked so wistful that Poseidon found himself wishing he *could* make that happen for her. But the only god with that kind of power was Zeus, and he didn't grant such favors lightly.

"Ooh! Look at all the people down there," Thetis exclaimed, suddenly cheerful again. They were flying over the country of Italy now, about a hundred feet or so above cozy villages, winding roads, and green hills. Having heard about the competition, mortals covered the hillsides and stood in village streets below, waving signs and cheering them on.

Thetis waved back, blowing kisses left and right. Poseidon was used to being adored by mortals—took it for granted, in fact—but her enthusiasm was catching.

"Hey, you're not excited or anything, are you?" he teased.

A long strand of turquoise hair had blown across

her cheek, and she pulled it away, tucking it behind one ear. "You bet your trident I am! Plus, everything is so beautiful from up here. I never realized. I guess it's nothing new to you, though."

She was right that it was nothing new. Still, seeing it all through her fresh eyes was kind of exhilarating. He was about to tell her so, when a voice called out.

"Hey! There you are!" Hades whizzed up in one of MOA's chariots with Delphinius and Pandora. The five of them flew side by side the rest of the way to Rome and landed at the Pantheon early that afternoon.

Athena's team had beaten them to it and was already heading up the building's front steps. And Ares' team was also just landing. Pandora and Thetis waved to them all.

Didn't they get that this was a contest? wondered Poseidon, feeling a little grumpy. You weren't supposed to be so friendly with other teams when you were trying to outdo them!

"Too bad we're not the first team to get here," Delphinius noted. Then he punched an encouraging fist in the air. "But we'll still win this thing!"

"Yeah!" shouted Pandora, high-fiving him.

"We'll outshine them all!" Thetis added, grinning.

Outshine? Poseidon eyed her suspiciously as he remembered the Oracle-O cookie fortune. Was her choice of words deliberate? Did she truly hope to *outshine* him? She didn't seem like a competitive type of person, but how well did he really know her? They hadn't hung around together all that long.

The relaxed feeling that had come over him during their trip vanished completely. He drew Thetis aside. "I meant to tell you—that was an awesome score back in Delphi. You coming up with the solution to the

Oracle's clue. But keep that kind of info just between the five of us from now on, okay? No need to give the other teams a heads-up."

She frowned at him. "If you say so."

Huh? He scowled at her. He'd just given her a compliment, in his own way. And that was good advice, whether she realized it or not. Sensing her disappointment in him, he said uncomfortably, "Well, see you inside." Then he rushed across the brick street to catch up to Hades and Delphinius and start up the steps of the Pantheon with them.

Pandora was already inside by now, her curious nature leading her to rush in ahead of the rest of them on the heels of Athena's team. Poseidon looked over one shoulder to be sure Thetis was coming too and felt relieved when he saw that she was. Though he wasn't sure how much he should trust her, she was still a member of his team. And he felt . . . well . . . *responsible* for her. Or something like that, anyway.

Eight granite columns that stood ten times as tall as the immortals fronted the Pantheon, with two more rows of four behind them. "They look like humongous soldiers guarding the temple's entrance," Hades commented as Thetis caught up to the three boys.

"Interesting observation," she said. "That kind of detail could help us with our first challenge here. Especially if it's another riddle."

"And they're Corinthian columns," Poseidon added quickly. "You can tell because they're decorated at the top with carved acanthus leaves."

Thetis smiled slightly, but Hades shot him a look that plainly said, *Duh, everyone knows that, god-dude.*

Poseidon immediately wished he could take back his comment. What was he doing—trying to impress

142

Thetis? Usually girls tried to impress *him*! For some reason he wanted her approval, though. Wanted her to think of him as a *good* guy and to look up to him.

After passing through a rectangular reception area, the students entered a massive round room that was topped with a concrete dome ceiling. At the dome's highest point, there was a circular opening. He could see sky through it.

Thetis pointed up at it. "The oculus."

"Now what?" said Pandora.

"Now we eat!" Delphinius said. His eyes had gone round with excitement, and he was pointing toward a long table across the room from where they were standing. Clay bowls decorated with black-silhouetted figures were laid out on it.

"That must be the food Zeus promised would be ready for us at each stop," Poseidon said. But his hungry team wasn't listening, for they had already started over to the table.

And indeed, the bowls were filled with favorite foods of the gods, he saw when he joined them. Yambrosia stew and ambrosia salads. Underworld stew, too (a traditional stew of potatoes, meat, and carrots, flavored with an Underworld plant called asphodel). Nectaroni and cheese. Celestial soup with noodles shaped like planets and stars. There were even cartons of nectar to drink.

But there were also Roman figs, dates, nuts, pears, grapes, cakes, and honey. Spying a note on the table beside the Roman treats, Poseidon picked it up. "The note's from the Roman caretakers of the Pantheon, thanking us for a crate of urns filled with Greek food."

"My dad must've had the urns delivered before we

got here," said Athena. "Probably to stimulate more cultural exchange. Few things make friendships form faster than sharing good food!"

Poseidon's team members eagerly grabbed plates and began to fill them. The scent of food was hard to resist. But he had his eye on the ultimate goal. *Winning* the games. It would be smart to poke around the Pantheon and get familiar with everything here now, *before* they were presented with their first real challenge.

"Food later; studying up on this place now," he called out to his team.

Delphinius froze, a forkful of nectaroni halfway to his mouth. "C'mon, god-dude. We're starving," he protested. "I mean, you're the best, but let's chill out and refuel."

"Everybody else is eating," Thetis pointed out.

And it was true. Most of the teams had arrived by now and were gathered around the table as well.

Ping. Ping. Ping. All the students cocked their heads at the sound.

"What was that?" asked Pandora.

"The MOA herald's lyrebell?" asked Hades.

"It's our scrolls," said Thetis, pulling hers out of the pocket of her scalloped golden chiton. "I think we all just got a message."

All over the Pantheon, students reached for their scroll-gadgets and unrolled them. The message had apparently come to everyone at once. Clever device Zeus had created, thought Poseidon. He pulled his purple team leader scroll from his pocket to read:

Chow now.

Your first challenge will come at noon.

—Zeus

"So I guess it's fine to go ahead and eat?" asked Pandora.

Poseidon nodded, giving up. "We've got an hour till noon."

"Yeah! You're the boss. Let's dig in!" said Delphinius. He wolfed down his nectaroni, then forked up another bite.

Once everyone on Poseidon's team had eaten their fill, they walked around to familiarize themselves with the temple. Hades and Delphinius even went outside again to scope out the exterior. Like Thetis had said, who knew what details might come in handy? The more information they had, the better!

Poseidon noticed Thetis gazing up at the ceiling and went over to her. "The distance from the ground up to the oculus measures the same as the width of the Pantheon's dome," she told him. "I read that in the sea scroll I told you about."

"Good fact. Might help us somehow," Poseidon approved. This girl was turning out to be almost as brainy as Athena, who often had her head in a book-scroll back at MOA.

Suddenly Thetis gasped.

"What's wrong?" Seeing that she was still looking up at the oculus, Poseidon looked up too. But all he saw through the opening was blue sky and puffy white clouds.

Thetis shook her head and then shrugged. "Uh, nothing, I guess. It's just . . . for a second, I thought I saw an eyeball looking down at us through the oculus."

"I'll wing up and check," said Poseidon. "Just in case there really *is* something on the roof. Might be some kind of clue!"

"Tell the others to keep surveying the area," he told her before he zoomed straight up and through the oculus in his winged sandals. When other team captains saw what he was up to, they did the same, wondering if he knew something they didn't.

Within seconds, Poseidon and five other captains were standing on the roof of the Pantheon, looking out over the city. Artemis was the only captain not among them, Poseidon noticed. Come to think of it, he hadn't seen her—or any of her team members, either—at the Pantheon yet.

"Why are we up here?" Medusa asked him point-blank. One of her immortal sisters had brought her up since she was mortal and couldn't make her winged sandals fly without help.

"For the view," Poseidon joked. Lifting a hand to shade his eyes, he gazed out over the surrounding rooftops and trees with pretended interest. The others followed his gaze, still thinking he must know something they didn't.

"Thetis didn't happen to share any more interesting information about this building, did she?" Apollo asked craftily.

"Maybe," said Poseidon, grinning. But he was really just looking around for anything out of the ordinary. He didn't spot a thing, though. Certainly nothing as weird as a big eyeball.

Athena was flying around the edge of the roof, studying it closely. No doubt, like him she was looking for details that might help her team in the coming challenge.

"Hey! Reporters and artists," Ares announced in delight. Sure enough, a group of mortals in the streets below were glancing up at them while busily taking notes or sketching on the scrolls they held.

"They must've heard that immortals were here," added Iris.

Feeling self-conscious, Poseidon lifted a hand to smooth back his hair. But it was already perfect, as usual. All three boy captains struck poses for the artists, trying to look as muscular as possible.

Mortal villagers gathered down there too, waving up at the captains. Some of the girls were blowing kisses and holding signs they'd made. One girl's sign read: Poseidon is Sea-rrific!

Ares grinned. "I bet Thetis agrees with that sign."

"Huh?" said Poseidon. "What do you mean?"

"She's your new crush, right?"

"No, she's not my—" Poseidon broke off to glance around at the others on the roof. They were all watching him now with expressions of amusement.

151

Was that what everyone thought? he wondered. Just because he'd given her a ride over and caught her when she was falling? "I barely know her," he said with a frown. "She's on my team. That's *all*."

"Don't be such a dripcompoop. Ares was just teasing," said Medusa.

Poseidon stiffened. He'd been called that and worse over the years, forever teased about his drippyness. "Ha-ha," he said. "Not."

If only he could let the teasing roll off his back—or maybe *drip* off his back—but he'd never been able to do that. He was constantly worried about what other students at the Academy thought of him. It was hard to measure up when you were competing with godboys like Ares, the god of war. Or with mortal boys like Heracles, who was the strongest mortal in the world.

And they weren't his only rivals at MOA. Apollo,

Dionysus, and Hephaestus—the list of their accomplishments was long and impressive. It was an uphill battle, trying to gain Zeus's notice with these other guys around. Kind of exhausting, actually.

But he was up to the challenge! Everyone knew that Zeus was totally into competitions. He was bound to be super impressed when Poseidon's team won the Temple Games.

With a flap of her small orange wings, Pheme sailed up through the oculus to join them on top of the roof. "Artemis's team went to Sicily by mistake," she announced. "They thought the first clue had something to do with Mr. Cyclops's home island. There's no way they could get here in time to win now. So her team is officially out of the race. I'll post the news to everyone's scrolls." With that, she dropped down through the oculus and into the Pantheon again.

"That's awful!" said Athena.

"Poor Artemis," groaned Iris.

Apollo looked disappointed. "I was wondering why I hadn't seen any of her team here. I was considering using our twin telepathy to try to find her if she didn't show soon." He and Artemis shared a kind of ESP that let them locate each other by bringing the other twin's image to mind.

No one liked to see a friend strike out, but that was the way competitions were, Poseidon thought. He felt sorry for Artemis and her team too, but he also couldn't help thinking *one down, five other teams to go!* Luckily, every team would win some kind of prize in the end, so it wasn't *that* awful of him to be kind of happy about Artemis's mistake, right?

Ping! Everyone's scrolls broadcasted the news

about Artemis. There was also a message from Zeus explaining their first challenge. It read:

Find the coffers.

Count their rings,

Times twenty-eight.

Minus the height of Pantheon

Plus the width of its dome.

(The use of winged sandals is not

allowed in this challenge.)

Everyone on the roof crammed back through the oculus to meet with their teams on the Pantheon floor. Each team huddled in a group, trying to figure out the answer to Zeus's riddle first.

Not far away, Poseidon heard Kydoimos on Ares' team whine, "Math? I thought these challenges would be games of skill. Ha!"

"Math *is* a skill," the Egyptian goddess Isis informed

him. The beads in her long hair clicked together as she shook her head at him scornfully.

"He meant the athletic kind of skill," his friend Makhai said hotly.

"Anyone have any *helpful* ideas on how we'll measure the height of this building without being able to use our sandals to fly up to the dome?" Ares butted in to ask his team.

Poseidon couldn't hear the rest, but smiled over what he had heard. Ares' sister Eris, the goddess of discord, seemed to be having her usual unsettling effect. Luckily, it was just Ares' team that was arguing so far.

"Okay," Poseidon said to his four teammates. "Any ideas?"

"Coffins are usually found in cemeteries, aren't they?" said Pandora.

"No, it was *coffers*, see?" said Thetis. She showed Pandora the words that Zeus had sent them on the scroll again.

"Coffers are like treasure chests," added Hades. "So they could have *rings* and other jewelry inside them."

"Then we just need to find the chests, open them, and count how many rings are inside," said Delphinius. "Easy peasy. Except for one thing. I didn't see any chests or trunks when I was looking around earlier. Did any of you?"

They all shook their heads. But a moment later Thetis's face lit up. "Hey, I just remembered that there's another meaning for coffers."

Poseidon raised his eyebrows. "Which is?"

"Those indented squares that cover the ceiling in here? *They're* called coffers," she explained. "And they're lined up in rows that circle this dome, just like big . . ."

157

"Rings?" Pandora gasped, and tilted her head to look up.

"Keep your head down," Poseidon growled at her and the others. "We don't want to give away the solution to this challenge before we've even figured it out ourselves." Without tilting his head, he raised his eyes upward. Visually counting, he said, "There are five rows, er, rings of those square coffer things. Everyone count the number of squares in each row. But try not to be obvious about it."

"We only need to count one row. All the rows have the same number," said Thetis. "See how they line up both ways, up *and* down?"

"She's right," said Delphinius. "They get smaller when the dome begins to curve higher, so the same number of coffers still fits in a ring."

"Uh-oh! Don't look now, but isn't Athena's team

staring at the ceiling too?" Pandora hissed. "They've probably figured out Zeus's clue too. Hurry!"

"I count twenty-eight squares in the bottom ring," said Hades. "Like Zeus's riddle."

"Twenty-eight times five. That's . . . ," said Thetis.

"One hundred and forty coffers," Poseidon said.

Delphinius clapped him on the back. "Is this guy good at math, or what? Now how do we figure out the height and width of the dome?"

Everyone looked at Thetis. "Well," she said. "I don't remember the measurements from the scroll-book I read. But like I told Poseidon, I do remember that the height and width are the same."

While they'd been talking, some of the other team members had found ropes in a storage closet along the Pantheon wall and rushed outside with them. "Since magic isn't allowed, they can't use their

159

winged sandals. So they'll probably climb the outer walls using those ropes," guessed Hades. "Then they'll drop the ropes down through the oculus to measure the distance to the floor. That'll all take a while."

"Think we should measure the width of the floor instead?" said Pandora.

"That would be easier and smarter. Good thing we're the only ones who know it measures the same as the ceiling height," said Delphinius.

He, Pandora, and Hades all started to step off the floor's width, heel to toe and heel to toe. Before they'd gone far, Poseidon and Thetis both exclaimed, "Wait!" at the exact same second, halting them in their tracks. Her eyes sparkled up at him with the knowledge that they'd both realized the same thing at the same time.

"We don't have to measure the floor or the ceiling," Poseidon told them in a low voice.

Thetis nodded. "Because they're the same. So no matter what they measure, subtracting one from the other like the clue says to do will cancel both out to zero. Which means that it's only the coffer count that, um, counts. So the answer to the challenge is . . ." She looked over at Poseidon, waiting.

"One hundred and forty!" he shouted.

Hearing this, Pheme jotted the number down on her scroll, sending it off to Zeus.

Almost immediately, all the teams' scrolls chimed *Ping! Ping!* When everyone checked them, they found the same message from Zeus. It read:

Congratulations!

Score one for Poseidon's team, winner of the first challenge.

5 rings of ceiling coffers x 28 coffers in a ring = 140 coffers

140 + (142 feet high − 142 feet wide) = 140

Next stop: The Temple of Uppsala in Sweden, for challenge two.

Good luck, teams!

You'll . . .

Suddenly, Zeus's message began to break up. A map to Uppsala appeared at the bottom of Poseidon's scroll, but the lines and labels on it were faint. He looked around and saw that everyone seemed to be having the same problem. Luckily, before the maps disappeared completely, he and the other captains were all able to trace the route to the next temple.

"I hope Zeus fixes those technical bugs soon," said Medusa. Her snakes nodded in agreement.

No other team was eliminated this round, since Artemis's had already been disqualified for showing up at the wrong place. Still, Poseidon had racked up the very first win, and others came by to congratulate him. It felt great! As the students who had been measuring outside filed in after learning the news of his team's win, each sent him a thumbs-up or came over to pay tribute to him.

"Let's get going," Poseidon told his team after a few minutes. "We don't want anyone else to—" He broke off when the Pantheon suddenly began shaking and quaking.

"It's happening again!" said Thetis, looking scared. "Just like at Delphi."

"A real earthquake this time?" Pandora asked, her eyes wide.

"No, it's the roof that's shaking, not the ground," called Athena, gazing upward.

"It sounds like ginormous feet are stomping around up there," said Iris.

Suddenly the pounding stopped. "Fee Fi Fo Fum! Fear us, Olympians. Here we come!" an army of deep voices shouted down from above.

Along with everyone else, Poseidon was looking up when a huge eyeball appeared and stared down at the students through the hole in the ceiling.

Thetis gasped. "Is that a . . . giant?"

7

Giant Trouble

Amphitrite

AMPHITRITE STUMBLED BACK IN SURPRISE AS actual giants began leaping through the oculus down into the Pantheon. There were five of them. *Boom! Boom! Boom! Boom! Boom!* Their feet hit the marble floor so hard that it shook when they landed.

Knocked off balance by the shaking, the students stumbled and bumped into one another, some falling to their knees. It was mass confusion!

"You okay?" asked a voice.

Amphitrite pushed back her hair to see Poseidon offering his hand. Though her legs had been getting stronger, they'd been no match for the wobbling floor, and she'd fallen. She nodded up at him as she took his hand, and he pulled her to stand.

"We're surrounded," one of the Chinese goddesses on Medusa's team murmured shakily.

Hearing the fear in her voice, Amphitrite reached out and gave her a hug, just like she would've done for one of her little sisters. She hoped Poseidon wouldn't mind her comforting members of an opposing team. After all, it seemed to her they had far bigger foes at the moment.

Namely giants! Their captors towered as tall as oak trees. They were big and bald, their bare feet covered in dirt like they'd just crawled out of the earth itself! They had long noses and hairy knuckles. But the really odd thing about them was the steam that curled up from the top of each giant's head like wild, wispy, constantly moving hair. Each sported a hairdo of a different color steam—pea green, orange, purple, yellow, and hot pink.

While blocking the way out of the Pantheon, the giants inched toward the students, corralling them into the very center of the room. They were trapped!

Athena pointed to the green-steam giant. "You stole my dad's omphalos!"

Amphitrite whipped around to see that the giant was indeed in possession of the stone egg from the Temple at Delphi. It sat atop his bald head like a crown. Steam funneled up from him, through the bottom end of the egg, and out through its top opening.

He grinned and thumped his chest with a big fist. "Me Prince Porphyrion. Egg mine. Me tell future from now on. Olympians' future look bad. Giants' future look *good*. Heh heh heh."

"What's that supposed to mean?" Medusa demanded. The snakes on her head were hissing and lunging wildly at the giants to no avail.

"Think that giant can really use the stone egg to see the future?" Pandora whispered to Amphitrite.

"Hope not," Amphitrite whispered back. "I think only the Oracle can do that—or could when she had the egg, anyway."

"If you give that omphalos back, we'll ask Zeus to go easy on your punishment," Athena commanded in a strong, clear voice.

The purple-steam giant shook his head and pointed at the green-steam giant, who seemed to be their leader. "Nuh-uh. Porphy like crown."

"Yeah," said the yellow-steam one. "Porphy gonna be king. Mommy say so."

At this, Ares started laughing. "King of what? Kindergarten?"

The giants all took a threatening step toward Ares and the other students, forcing them to draw into a tighter group. For a few seconds, the oculus threw light on the omphalos, and Amphitrite noticed something she hadn't back in the Oracle's dim sanctuary. The carved net design that covered the egg had glossy, gleaming little bumps all along it. They were spaced evenly, one on each carved knot.

And the bumps caught the sunlight whenever the giant moved his head. She squinted, trying to see them better. Was it possible . . . were those bumps actually *pearls* embedded along the knots in the carved rope? Could this carefully designed geo-metric pattern that resembled a net actually be the legendary string of pearls?

A thrilling hope shot through her. She felt in her pocket for the pearl she'd found in the Oracle's sanctuary back in Delphi. It was still there. Had it popped off the omphalos when the giant's fist had grabbed it? She wondered how she could get close enough to see for herself without getting clobbered by one of these grumpy-looking giants.

"No!" Porphy raged. "We not in kindeegarten. School *dumb*. Me gonna be king of the wor—" he started to say.

But then a new voice interrupted him from out of nowhere. A woman's voice, though she wasn't visible. "Zeus knooows we have the omphalos. And he is pow-erless to stop whaaat I have planned," she crooned.

"What? I—I don't believe you," Athena said in a worried voice. "Who are you? And where are you?"

"I know that voice," hissed Iris from somewhere inside the group of students. "It's Gaia!"

Hades nodded. "Yeah. I think her voice is coming from that stone egg. She must've shape-shifted into something small enough to fit inside it."

Then the voice became so quiet the students could no longer make out what it was saying. Porphy cocked his head as if to listen better. "Okay, Mommy," he replied, and reached toward Pheme. With a hairy finger and thumb, he plucked the only two-way-communication scroll the Olympians had right out of her hands.

"Hey! I need that!" she protested.

Porphy and his giant pals ignored her and got busy turning the scroll-gadget upside-down and shaking it like a rattle, trying to figure out how it worked.

"Someone's got to escape to MOA to let Zeus know what's happening," Poseidon said in a low voice.

"I'll do it," Iris offered. Quickly she wound up a ball of magic and pitched it high overhead. Only instead of a ball, she tossed out a rainbow for transportation. *Brrrng!* It arced high, hurtling toward the oculus.

But the orange-steam giant simply raised one meaty hand. He caught the ball of rainbow magic Iris had thrown and squashed it into nothingness. *Pfft!*

"So much for me getting word to Zeus," said Iris, her shoulders drooping.

Thunk! Porphy had finally given up on the two-way-communication scroll and dropped it into the hole at the top of the egg.

"Why are you bugging us like this?" Pandora dared

to shout up at Gaia. "What did we ever do to you?"

"Glad you asked," Gaia's disembodied—or rather, *egg*-embodied—voice replied after a minute. "I've been stewing over Zeus's imprisonment of my son, Typhon. I figure if you Olympians can butt into my boys' business, *we* can butt into your competition."

Astonished, anxious murmurs rose from the students at this, but Gaia talked on. "I've sent Zeus a message just now on this amusing little scroll-gadget. He's already replied, agreeing to let my five boys join in the Temple Games as a new team."

"No way!" Eros began.

"Liar!" someone else called.

"These are *our* games. I say we battle these giants here and now!" shouted Ares, taking a fighting stance.

"Inadvisable," said Gaia in voice that was eerie for its calmness. "Because I have one hundred giant sons in all. And if you don't let my boys compete, their brothers will come. Think of it as a hundred Typhons let loose on the world."

An unhappy silence settled over the students.

Amphitrite scanned her team's faces. "The hundred fighters the Oracle mentioned?" she asked worriedly. Poseidon sent her a grim look. No wonder Gaia was acting so sure of herself, Amphitrite thought. Even Ares—god of war—wouldn't be able to fight off a hundred giants!

"Ah, I see you finally understand things," Gaia gloated. "All I'm asking is that you give my boys the same hope as you. The chance to win a temple built in their honor. Is that so wrong?"

"I don't trust her," Amphitrite whispered to Poseidon.

"Me neither," he agreed, nodding.

Suddenly, the scroll-gadget came hurtling down

to Pheme again. She caught it and scanned its current message. "It's true," she told everyone. "Zeus *has* agreed to let these five giants compete."

"Good, that's settled, then." Gaia cackled gleefully. "The competition will continue, and Zeus will provide me with my own two-way scroll-gadget for the rest of the games. However, since the rules say there can be only six teams by this point in the competition, I'm afraid one of your teams will have to drop out. Iris's team."

"What? That isn't fair!" complained Zephyr. Other students also began grumbling in dismay.

"Is too fair," said Porphy. He crossed his arms, which looked as thick and strong as the columns that stood around Mount Olympus Academy. "Iris mean to our brother Typhon. Iris out. Giants in. Or . . . deal off. Right, Mommy?"

"Right," cooed Gaia's voice. "And we all heard you try to bail out of the competition a few minutes ago. An automatic out. Rules are rules."

Frowning deeply, Iris nevertheless nodded. "I'll find Artemis," she said quietly to those around her. "We won't be far behind you, wherever you go. We'll watch for a chance to help."

Brrrng! Iris tossed out a new rainbow. None of the giants attempted to stop this one, though. It arced high, forming a trail of colors that shot up through the oculus and off into the distance. The other five teams watched helplessly as Iris, Aglaia, Hephaestus, Zephyr, and Boreas headed out across it.

"Zeus and I have agreed to keep our distance from the game from this point on, so I must go. Good luck, sweet giants. Let the games continue!" Gaia shouted cheerfully. A ball of dust and vines shot from Porphy's head and up through the oculus, taking the giants' mom with it.

"There she blows," muttered Hades.

What had she gotten herself into? wondered Amphitrite. Yesterday she'd been safe, though maybe a little bit bored, at home in the Aegean Sea. And now she was in a dangerous contest against a team of giants!

"Let's beat it to the Temple of Uppsala in Sweden!" Poseidon shouted.

"Before these giant buttinskies can get there first," seconded Medusa.

"Yeah!" added Athena.

Ares punched a fist in the air, and Heracles raised his club. "You said it!" they yelled.

Buoyed by the determination of those around her, Amphitrite shouted, "Let's go!" Together their teams would fight these giant bullies. No way would they be allowed to win the games!

Feeling feisty and fierce, all twenty-five remaining students raced around and between the giants' legs, heading for the Pantheon's door. However, in three giant steps, the giants ducked out the door first. Slamming it shut behind them, they locked the students inside.

"Those big guys are fast!" exclaimed Apollo.

"Listen! What's that horrible sound?" said Medusa, shushing everyone. They all quieted at once. From outside came loud, crunching sounds.

"Something's being destroyed out there," said Pheme.

Poseidon pointed to the oculus. "Up and away!" He took Amphitrite's hand and whooshed upward. After all, now that the challenge was over, so was the ban on using winged sandals.

Without worrying about who was on whose team,

the remaining immortals helped the mortal students to wing up to the Pantheon's roof as well. Athena took Heracles' hand, and Dionysus grasped Medusa's. In this moment, there were no divisions. They were like one steadfast team, united against a single *giant* foe.

As they stood atop the roof outside, a terrible sight greeted their eyes. Their carts and chariots had been crushed to smithereens down in the street.

"Those giants stomped our transport!" Hades said darkly.

"Luckily, we can do without if we must. Onward!" said Athena. With that, the students took off, zooming northward to Sweden on winged sandals.

Once they were flying high above the giants, Poseidon glanced at Amphitrite. "Know anything about Uppsala?"

"No, unfortunately," she admitted. "None of the scrolls

in the MUMS library mentioned it." Below them, she caught a glimpse of the giants. They were running the whole way, their big feet splashing through lakes and seas and smashing down trees in forests.

"No worries," Poseidon replied. "We'll still beat these giants. I mean, Fee Fi Fo Fum, we are smart and they are dumb, right?"

A surprised giggle burst from her. "I can't believe how calm you are. Is this a typical day for you Olympians? I mean, being attacked and stuff?"

He shrugged, then grinned. "Guess so. Some days are more action-packed than others. You seem to be rolling with it, though."

"Well, it's not what I would have exactly hoped for, but . . ." Hearing shouts, she looked down.

Below them, cheering crowds had gathered in cities and farmlands. Keeping a wary eye out for the giants, the mortal well-wishers waved signs and called encouragements skyward as the students passed over them. Their signs said things like: *Immortals Rule! Beat Those Giants! Yay, MOA!*

"Look, they're all rooting for us. Word of what's happening has really spread fast," Amphitrite mused. She glanced sideways to see Pheme writing on her two-way scroll-gadget as her small orange wings kept her aloft and moving forward.

Poseidon looked down at the signs and nodded. "Hermes delivered those scroll-gadgets to every realm in the world. Pheme's the best at spreading news, so it's a sure thing everyone knows what's up. And they know what danger they could be in if the giants win."

"I never realized how much mortals depend on you . . . on all immortals, I mean," said Amphitrite.

Poseidon nodded. "If the giants win a temple,

they'll gain status. No one wants to have to worship them. They must be stopped."

"What . . . what if we fail?" Amphitrite murmured. "If they beat us, they might grow bold enough to start trampling creatures all over the world! Including my family in the Undersea."

"Hey! Have no fear. We may have to play along with those giant dweebs for now, but we'll get 'em in the end. In this to win this, remember?"

"Are you just trying to cheer me up?" she asked, sending him a sideways glance.

He grinned back at her. "Is it working?"

She laughed, feeling greatly encouraged by his faith in the students' ability to crush the formidable power of their giant foes. "Yes!"

By four o'clock, they found themselves over Sweden, flying above bright green hills dotted with sheep. Soon they were approaching the temple of Uppsala, which looked like a beautiful castle with turrets. A splendid tree and a water well stood alongside the temple.

"It's so pretty!" she said enthusiastically. "But what's that sparkling band wrapped around the temple's turrets?"

"Looks like some kind of chain," Poseidon said as they drew nearer.

He was right. It was indeed a chain. With huge golden links that encircled the temple's turrets. What could it be for? Minutes after they landed under the tree next to the temple, the other four remaining student teams also set down. Luckily, the giants hadn't been able to run as fast as the students' winged sandals could fly, but Gaia's boys weren't far behind.

Hearing a clacking sound, which seemed to be coming from the tree, Amphitrite stepped closer to it.

Long green vines trailed from its branches to sweep the ground. And there was something else, too.

"How weird!" she said, pointing up into its branches. Nine marionettes, each about as big as she was, hung high in the tree on puppeteer strings. They were carved from wood and had painted faces, hair, and clothing. Their wooden legs and arms clicked and clacked against each other whenever a breeze blew.

"Where did those come from?" asked Pandora, gazing up at them too. "Is that a weird tree, or what?"

"We are hung in this tree every nine years during a great festival," said a clacky voice. The marionettes could speak!

"This tree is a very special tree with wide-spread branches, always green in both winter and summer. What kind it is, nobody knows," a second marionette informed them.

After each finished speaking, it mysteriously disappeared into thin air. *Poof! Poof!* Now there were seven left in the tree.

"So do you marionettes all talk?" asked Pandora.

"Yes," said a third marionette. *Poof!* It was gone too.

"That was a useless question," Poseidon scolded. "It's pretty clear they can all talk, and furthermore, that they'll only answer one question apiece before disappearing. So let's think about what we might need to know to win this challenge and only ask questions about that."

Pandora looked a bit embarrassed, but nodded. Amphitrite's heart twisted a little in sympathy. However, Poseidon seemed oblivious to the fact that he'd hurt the mortal girl's feelings.

"What's our challenge, if you know it?" Athena asked yet another marionette. Unfortunately, just as she asked this, the giants arrived. Though breathless from running, there was nothing wrong with their ears, and they heard the marionette's answer too.

"Simply pick up the small ancient stone, called a rune, which sits upon the center of the temple roof. But you must do so without touching the roof itself," said the marionette. *Poof!* Now only five marionettes were left.

Instantly, Ares, Apollo, and some other students raced over to begin climbing the temple walls, aiming for the roof. The giants were faster. They grabbed the chain links that ran along the top of the temple, preparing to leap over them.

"What happens if we *do* touch the temple's roof?" Pandora blurted. This earned her a dark look from Poseidon.

Amphitrite spoke up quickly, "Good question. I'd like to know the answer too." The giants and immortals who'd started climbing obviously wanted to hear the answer also, because they paused and looked over at the marionettes.

"If you touch the roof, you'll turn into a newt," said the marionette. *Poof!* That left only four of them.

Looking wary now, the giants backed away from the temple. The students did too. If any of them turned into a newt, they'd have to drop out of the competition. And, well, they'd be a *newt*.

"What now?" Eris asked. When another marionette opened its jaws to speak, she turned on it. "Not you! I wasn't asking you. I was talking to the other teams."

But it was too late. "*Now* you must figure out how to complete the challenge," the marionette told her. *Poof!* Three of them were left.

"Duh! Don't we know that already?" asked the giant with orange steam coming from the top of his head.

"Yes." *Poof!* Now only two marionettes remained. Porphy and the others jumped on the orange-steam giant, pummeling him for wasting a question.

"Wait! I know!" Apollo said to the other students. "From now on, let's discuss questions before we officially ask them."

This idea was agreed upon, and various suggestions about what to ask were made. "Let's ask them how to successfully complete the challenge," Amphitrite put in.

"Good one," said Poseidon. The rest of the team members nodded approval, so she put the question to the marionettes. Unfortunately, there seemed to be no way of preventing the giants from also hearing the answer. But as it turned out, that didn't matter.

"That is one question we cannot answer," said one of the two remaining marionettes. "You must figure it out for yourself," said the other. Since they couldn't give an answer, neither of them poofed away.

"I have another idea," said Amphitrite. "But . . ." She tossed her head toward the listening giants.

Pheme took the hint that she didn't want the giants to overhear her idea. "Hey, giants?" Pheme called to them. "I think the world needs to learn more about you guys. Come over here for an interview that'll make you famous!" Looking excited, the giants gathered around her a ways off.

Meanwhile, Amphitrite waved the other students closer and whispered her plan. "It involves climbing trees, shooting arrows, and walking tightropes. I'm no good at any of those things, so I hope some of you are."

"Go on," said Poseidon.

She did, and after she explained everything, the students broke from their huddle. Immediately,

Poseidon shinnied up the tree and whispered in a marionette's ear. Seeing this, the giants broke away from Pheme to see what he was up to.

"Fifty feet," the marionette replied loudly, in answer to Poseidon's question. *Poof!* Now only one puppet remained.

"Hey!" complained Porphy. Green steam pumped angrily from his stone-egg crown. "No fair. We not hear question."

"Poseidon asked how many feet twenty-five giants have," Isis fibbed quickly.

"Oh," said the giant. But he frowned as if he suspected he was being tricked.

Which he was, Amphitrite knew. Because all five student teams were in on her plan, and Isis's fib was part of it. Students began pulling vines from the tree and tying them together to form a rope.

One that was way longer than fifty feet.

The giants could only look on in confusion. "This challenge is going to take a while," Medusa explained with her fingers crossed behind her back. "So we're weaving hammocks in case we have to sleep here overnight."

Although it wasn't true, the giants seemed to buy it. Next, Ares' and Athena's teams announced that they were each going to walk around the temple and meet on its far side to try to figure out another way to get the rune. As they'd hoped, the giants insisted on tagging along. It was all part of the crafty plan Amphitrite had come up with.

While the giants were gone, the vine rope was completed and looped into a coil for easy carrying. Apollo took the coil with him and climbed onto a high branch. After tying one end of the vine securely to the tree, he stood on the branch and pulled a golden arrow from the quiver he wore. He drew it in his bow, took careful aim, and fired.

"Quick as a wink, fly through two links!" he commanded. His arrows were magical, and this one played a happy tune as it flew through the air to do his bidding.

Whoosh! The arrow shot through the hole in the nearest link of the chain that encircled the top of the temple's turrets. It was a blur as it continued onward through another chain link on the opposite side of the roof, just as if it were threading a needle. Amazing!

"Good shot! Got it!" Ares' voice called out from the far side of the temple. The knotted vine now stretched from the tree through a link above the roof of the temple from one side to the other through another link, and down to Ares and the others on the ground.

Apollo shinnied down the tree and Poseidon climbed up. All eyes were glued to Poseidon, everyone holding their breath as they watched the plan unfold. Even the last marionette looked on in fascination as Poseidon grabbed onto the taut vine. Hand over hand, he began pulling himself along it, his legs dangling in midair below.

Within minutes, he was hanging from the vine just above the center of the roof. Hooking the back of his knees over the vine, he flipped to momentarily hang upside down. Amphitrite clasped her hands tight, seriously hoping that this brave godboy wouldn't wind up a newt. Grabbing the small stone rune from the middle of the roof, Poseidon then righted himself, tucked the rune into his pocket, and returned on the vine to the others, victorious.

"Score!" he crowed. He hopped off the branch and held out his palm, displaying the rune to them all.

"That was amazing!" said Amphitrite.

As others offered him their congratulations, they all studied the strange markings on the rune, wondering what they meant. Before their eyes, the markings quickly rearranged themselves into the words: *Go to the city that is not allowed.* Then the rune leaped from his palm and flew back to lie on the center of the castle roof again.

"It must be our next clue!" said Athena.

Seeing all this, Pheme jotted a message on her scroll, sending it off to Zeus. Almost immediately, all the teams' scrolls chimed, *Ping! Ping!* When everyone checked them, they found the same message from Zeus. And one from Gaia, too.

Pheme read both messages aloud.

"Zeus writes, 'Well done students!'"

"Gaia writes back, 'They did not play fair! Your students banded together.'"

"Yeah, that's thirty-eight against four," Porphy put in. Of course, he'd gotten the numbers all wrong. There were only twenty-five students left in the competition. And when he'd counted his own team members, he'd forgotten to add himself in to make five.

"Now Gaia writes, 'I demand that Ares' team be eliminated for bad sportsmanship,'" read Pheme.

"Yeah!" The giants all glared at Makhai and Kydoimos from Ares' team.

"Did those two do something against the rules to help us win?" Pandora asked the students nearby.

Heracles nodded, smiling. "When we were on the other side of the castle, they *accidentally* shot arrows at the giants. Nailed them in the . . ."

"But . . . that wasn't Ares' fault!" Hades yelled out.

"Yeah! You don't think it was bad sportsmanship for your team to crush our carts and chariots outside the Pantheon?" Ares huffed at the giants in his team's defense.

"He's right!" said his sister Eris. "Uh-huh!" agreed his teammate Isis. "Can't we all just get along?" Harmonia said, trying to maintain peace and harmony.

Pheme looked up from her scroll-gadget. "Zeus has declared Apollo's team the winner of this challenge because he provided the crucial archery skill that made Amphitrite's plan possible, stringing the vine that allowed Poseidon to get the rune."

Amphitrite was surprised at the decision since Poseidon had been the one to actually risk becoming a newt when he'd plucked the rune from the castle roof. Really, it had been a team effort, though, so choosing one winner couldn't have been easy for Zeus. Amphitrite could see from the mix of emotions flitting across Poseidon's face that he was trying to accept Zeus's ruling. Good for him. She sent him a supportive smile.

"And Ares' team is officially eliminated," said Pheme. "That is final. Ares, remove your team from the playing field."

Looking reluctant but resigned, Ares and his team released the silver wings on their sandals and rose to hover a few inches in the air. Since Isis didn't have winged sandals, she held Eris's hand.

"We'll be watching on our scrolls and rooting for you. Shout if you need our help," Amphitrite heard Ares murmur to Poseidon.

Then Ares and his team took off. "Good luck!" they called back to the remaining four teams led by Athena, Poseidon, Apollo, and Medusa.

There was an unhappy silence among the students after Ares' team left, but the giants were grinning. Then, Heracles shouted, "Let's win this thing!" Cheers greeted his determined cry.

Pandora scrunched up her nose in confusion. "But how? Where's the city that's not allowed?" Which was exactly what Amphitrite had been wondering.

The last marionette's wooden bones rattled in the wind, then it answered. "As the rune instructed, you must now proceed to the *Forbidden City* in China to face another challenge in the Temple of Heaven," it told them. "But first, you need sleep."

Athena snapped her fingers. "So that's it. *Forbidden*. As in *not allowed*."

As the puppet *poofed* into nothingness, a jagged white streak lit up the sky. Then, *Ka-BOOM!* It was followed by a crash of thunder. The students and the giants all looked up as a second bolt of lightning hit a group of clouds above them. In an instant the slug grew dark. A light snow began to fall, drifting down to cover the ground.

"Look! Someone—probably Zeus—has drawn a map for us in the snow," said Amphitrite. She pointed at a big dot on the map. "And I'm guessing that's the Forbidden City. As she and the others studied it, she yawned, feeling suddenly exhausted.

"This is not normal snow," she heard someone say.

Amphitrite nodded. "Yeah. It's not even cold or anything. I think it's some kind of magic to make us all go to—"

But before she could finish, she, the other students, and the giants, too, all dropped off to sleep.

8

More Challenges

Poseidon

"THE GIANTS ARE GONE!" SOMEONE SHOUTED early the next morning.

"Whah?" Poseidon sat up and stretched. He'd been sleeping on the ground under the strange tree at Uppsala. Instantly recalling all that had happened the previous day, he jumped to his feet. The magic snow and its map had disappeared.

He remembered the directions to the Temple of Heaven well enough to get there, though. Did his competitors? Since he still hoped to win a temple in his name when the games were over, he wouldn't exactly be sorry if they'd forgotten the directions and wound up getting lost. He was glad the student teams had pulled together to defeat the giants in yesterday's challenge, but he was still smarting from Apollo's team having been given credit for the win.

"Think those giants decided to quit and go home?" Pandora wondered aloud.

"I seriously doubt it," scoffed Medusa's sister Stheno.

"Get up, everyone!" yelled Delphinius. "The giants have gotten a head start on us."

"I'm starving," said Actaeon, one of the mortals on Apollo's team.

"Look up," Thetis said, pointing overhead. "That tree grew fruit overnight!" She'd been sitting on the tree's roots, combing her long turquoise hair. Now she stowed the comb in her scalloped chiton's pocket, and they all began picking the low-hanging fruit she'd spotted.

A few minutes later, Poseidon felt a hand slide into his. It was hers. She smiled and handed him an apple. Then they all winged up and away in their magical sandals, munching the only breakfast they would have. He'd been a little worried that she might actually *outshine* him yesterday with her arrow-through-the-vine plan. But she hadn't tried to do any such thing. She'd been a real team player. Maybe that Oracle-O cookie hadn't known what it was talking about after all.

"The temples in the competition have all been lined up in a clockwise direction so far, have you noticed?" Thetis said to him as they flew. "So I'm guessing the rest of the temples after the Forbidden City will be in countries between China and Greece."

"Maybe the sixth and final one will be in Greece itself," said Poseidon. One of the ribbons he'd pinned to his tunic blew upward, tickling his neck. He pressed a hand over it, smoothing it down.

"Why do you wear all those things? Are they medals?" Thetis asked, gesturing the apple she held toward all the ribbons and pins on his tunic.

"They're favors. For luck." Poseidon nodded toward the mortal boy who was winging along just ahead of them, his hand holding Athena's. "See how Heracles is wearing an owl pin on his lion-skin cape? That's one of Athena's goddess symbols. She loaned that pin to him for the games, and he gave her that lion pin she's wearing."

"And over there? See that flash of gold at Dionysus's neck? The necklace with a charm hanging from it? It's not really his style, but he wore it because Medusa gave it to him for luck. And she's wearing a sprig of grapevine he gave her.

"And I'm pretty sure that orange ribbon on Eros's tunic is a gift from Pheme. Orange is her favorite color. They're all favors students have traded. To lend each other luck and protection."

"Who gave you all the ones you have?" Thetis asked, her eyes going wide as she surveyed the number he wore. She took a last bite of her apple, then tossed its core away to fall into a forest they were passing over.

"Fans," he told her, tossing his core after hers. "Mortals, mainly." He didn't add that they were mostly from girls. Girls he didn't even know. For

204

the first time ever, he wished that someone he cared about—or at least knew well—had sent him even a single one of the favors he wore.

Thetis cocked her head at him, her eyes on his face. As if she'd guessed his thoughts. Which made him feel weirdly embarrassed.

He didn't want her to know how lonely he sometimes felt. He didn't want her to feel sorry for him. He needed to get a grip, or he was going to lose his focus. Maybe even lose the games! And get crushed by giants, too.

He flashed her his patented cute-guy smile. "Mortals are always sending small gifts to the immortals on Mount Olympus," he said in a confident voice. "You know how it is."

"Not really," she said. "That's never happened to me."

What was she thinking now? he wondered when

she fell silent. He almost asked, but then Delphinius and Hades winged over, with Pandora between them. The five of them traveled the rest of the way to China as a group, discussing the competition and all that had happened.

By noon that day they found themselves hovering over the Forbidden City. It stood within a bigger complex and was not only protected by a wall, but by water-filled moats!

"I hope our challenge isn't that we have to break into that city," said Hades, eyeing the fortifications dubiously.

Poseidon shook his head, picturing the snow map from the night before in his mind. "I think that's the Temple of Heaven over there, outside the walls of the Forbidden City," he told them, pointing. The temple was big, round, brightly painted in reds and golds, and had three circular blue roofs stacked one floor above the other, pagoda-style. The center of the uppermost roof rose to a point topped with a round gold knob. Nearby were flower gardens, fountains, and a bell tower.

A group of mortal girls were hanging around the gardens. They shrieked with joy upon seeing the immortals land. "Poseidon!" One girl ran over to him. Jumping up and down, she thrust out a scroll. "Would you sign my scrollbook?"

"Mine too!" "Mine too!" pleaded the other girls.

"Sure," Poseidon said in a smooth, assured voice. It was easy to slip back into the role he was used to. Admired godboy of MOA. But after a minute he looked around. "Thetis?"

"I'm here," she said with a sigh. She was behind him. "The others went inside already. If you can tear yourself away from your fans, maybe we should go inside too? I thought you wanted to beat those giants!"

Whoa, thought Poseidon. She sounded a little ticked off. What was her hurry all of a sudden? Then it struck him. Could she be a tiny bit *jealous* of those other girls' attention? That had to be it. Which must mean she *liked* him, he thought happily. "Sorry, gotta go now," he said to his girl fans. Then he followed Thetis inside the temple.

Two Chinese girl guides about their same age welcomed them. Both wore shiny red robes with bell-shaped sleeves and wide gold belts. They led his team into a circular room with numerous tall red columns, where the other competitors waited. The other four teams (including the giants) were gathered around tables set with clay bowls.

Poseidon, Thetis, and their team took seats on low

pillows around the table reserved for them. Then they dug in to the delicious food set before them. The bowls were heaped with a variety of Chinese delicacies, such as stir-fried rice with egg and vegetables. There was nectar to drink as well.

The bowls on the giants' table were enormous, and they were eating with their hands and licking their fingers.

"Eew?" Pandora commented, shaking her head at them.

"Definitely eew," Thetis replied, nodding.

"Welcome to the Temple of Heaven," the Chinese guides began. "Let us tell you something about this place. Since the sky and the heavens are blue, the three roofs of this temple are painted blue to match."

Poseidon noticed that the guides kept smiling at Wen Chi and Mazu, the Chinese goddesses on

Medusa's team, as they spoke about the temple. He frowned. Would Medusa's team have a leg up on everyone else because of what those two girls must already know about this temple?

"Twice a year the emperor leaves the Forbidden City to perform a ceremony here in the Temple of Heaven. Each step in this ceremony must be completed perfectly to ensure a good harvest for the crops in China," one of the guides said. "The smallest mistake in the ceremony is a bad omen for our country."

"But what is new challenge?" demanded Porphy, impatiently cutting into the girl's speech. His four giant brothers grunted their approval of his question.

Thetis and some of the other students frowned at the giants' rudeness, but Poseidon was in agreement with those giants for once. He'd finished eating and was more than ready to get on with the competition.

"We will move on, then," said one the guides. She spoke in a pleasant tone, seeming not to have taken offense at the giant's interruption. "As part of your challenge, you all must now learn the steps in the traditional Chinese tea ceremony."

The guides began to clear the clay food bowls from each table, replacing them with blue-and-white teapots and cups, a bamboo scoop, a large bowl of water, a canister of oolong tea leaves, a strainer, and other tools. Each competitor received a tray containing these items, all carefully positioned just so.

"Huh?" muttered Hades, staring doubtfully at the tray before him. "We spent weeks working out on obstacle courses and getting in shape for the games. And now our challenge is making *tea*?"

Though Poseidon felt the same way, Hades' comment

struck him as funny and he laughed, forgetting his impatience for the moment. He'd hoped for a challenge involving water, but making tea wasn't exactly the water-based challenge he'd envisioned, he thought wryly.

He wasn't the only one giggling. Seeing the giants with delicate China cups as tiny as thimbles in their fingers proved a total crack-up to all of the students.

There turned out to be numerous steps to the tea ceremony, an act said to bring wealth and happiness. For a while it was mostly moving hot water from one small cup to another, as tea leaves steeped in a tiny teapot. Eventually, however, each competitor wound up with a small steaming cup of tea. Even the giants managed to do this more or less successfully.

"Who won?" asked Pandora as she started to take a drink.

"Wait!" cautioned one of the Chinese guides. "The challenge has not ended."

"It has only just begun! Now you must all stand, take your full cup of tea outside, and place it atop your head. Then you must walk one lap around the exterior walls of the Forbidden City complex and return here," added the second Chinese guide. "All without spilling any tea. First person to return wins for their team."

The students jumped up eagerly. "Be careful," the two Chinese guides called after them. "If you spill even a single drop of tea, your team will be disqualified! But if no team is disqualified, last team back is out."

Poseidon gathered his team together and helped them steady their teacups atop their heads. After they took off walking, he finger-combed his own hair

213

flat and set his cup on his head. Then he followed close behind his team.

Pandora was the weak link among them, he quickly realized. She kept turning her head this way and that to stare at anything she found curious— long silk scrolls hanging on the exterior walls of the Forbidden City, a red lacquer throne passing by on a litter carried by men in white, two ladies wearing richly embroidered gowns.

Just when Poseidon was about to blow his top at her, Thetis stepped in, gently directing her to focus. "Keep looking straight ahead, Pandora. You'll still be able to see things from the corners of your eyes. Good work. Keep going. We're almost a quarter of the way around!"

"Nicely done," Poseidon whispered as he fell in step with his mergirl teammate.

"Thanks." She smiled over at him as they kept a careful but brisk pace. "It's all that seal herding my sister Thetis and I do in the Undersea."

"You mean you and your little sister, Thetis Two?" he asked.

"Huh?" She jerked in surprise, causing tea to slosh in her cup.

"Hey, careful," he cautioned.

"Yes. I mean, sorry. My little sister. That's what I meant to say."

Crash! Hearing someone's teacup bite the dust behind him, Poseidon didn't dare look back for fear he'd unsettle his own cup.

"Uh-oh, someone's out," Delphinius said a few steps ahead of them.

"Wasn't anyone on our team, though. Just keep an eye on Pandora," advised Poseidon.

"You know, maybe you shouldn't be quite so hard on her," Thetis said from beside him. "She actually got some good information from those marionettes in Uppsala. If you give us all a chance to show what we can do, we might surprise you."

Poseidon turned his head slightly to follow Thetis as she moved up to walk alongside Pandora, who'd gotten distracted again. He didn't like to admit it, but maybe she was right. Pandora *had* asked a good question or two back in Uppsala. And sometimes he did overlook how others felt in his drive to be top godboy. Maybe he *should* try to offer his team more encouragement.

In an effort to do just that, he began to coach Pandora as they walked along. "Good posture. Steady going. Focus," he said. He was surprised at how pleased she seemed at the positive attention. It kind of made him feel good too.

They were back in the courtyard at the finish line before he knew it. But due to their longer strides, the giants had returned to the starting point ahead of everyone else. The tiny teacups had fit perfectly in the steam blowholes atop their heads, anchoring them snugly the whole race. They hadn't spilled a single drop of tea. And the steam had even kept theirs hot!

The crash they'd all heard earlier had been Medusa's cup hitting the path. She was out, and the giants had won the competition! No one was happy about this outcome, especially Medusa and her snakes, which hissed at the giants.

"That green-steam giant tripped me and made me drop my cup," she complained. This news did nothing to bolster student goodwill toward the giants, of course. Although Medusa's snakes had always kind of icked Poseidon out, right now he felt like hissing at the giants on her behalf too!

It was the giant's word against Medusa's, since no one else had seen what had happened. And since the giants denied any wrongdoing, Zeus had no choice but to send his confirmation of their win by scroll-gadget. He didn't seem happy about it either, for his message was curt. Afterward, the guides handed Pheme an Oracle-O cookie, then bowed farewell to the students before retreating into the Temple of Heaven.

Pheme stood on the temple steps and opened the cookie, which broadcasted its instructions to the students loud and clear: "Proceed to India and visit Badrinath, a Hindu temple dedicated to Lord Vishnu in the Himalayan Mountains. There, one team will triumph and yet another be eliminated."

Since India bordered China, this trip took less than an hour in giant steps and by winged sandal. Soon the teams were assembled together in the craggy mountains before a temple painted in yellows, blues, and reds. It had flags flying from above, a large bell at its entrance, and a hot sulfur spring bubbling below.

Right away, a woman wearing a colorful sari greeted them. When the girls oohed and ahhed over it, she informed them that it was one long piece of cloth wrapped in a special way to create a gown. It kind of resembled the chitons the goddessgirls at MOA wore, thought Poseidon, only with even more decoration.

"According to Hindu legend, the Indian god Vishnu visited Badrinath to meditate," the lady guide told them. She gestured toward a life-size gilded stone statue of the god, which stood beside her.

"Whoa! Did you count those arms? He has six!" said Pandora.

The guide nodded. "Lord Vishnu is often shown with multiple arms to demonstrate his superhuman power and his ability to perform several acts at once. Which brings me to your challenge."

As she paused, the students and giants all leaned in, their interest rising. They could hardly wait to hear what their challenge would be!

"Like Vishnu, you will have to perform numerous actions at once in this challenge," she went on. "As each person makes mistakes, they will step out of the competition. The first team with all its members out is eliminated. The last person standing wins for her or his entire team."

"Now we begin. First, you must all stand on one

leg," their guide instructed. Giggles rippled over the group as she waited for everyone to do so. Centaur, from Apollo's team, was allowed to stand on three legs, since he had four. Then she went on, "At the same time, you must also tap your heads with one hand and rub your stomachs with your other hand."

Once everyone was doing these three tasks simultaneously, she said, "Now nod your head as well."

Poseidon couldn't help grinning as she went on adding more actions. Others were laughing outright. They all looked and felt ridiculous, but after all the tensions of the competition, it was kind of fun!

"This reminds me of sunning," said Thetis as she hopped on one foot beside him. When the others nearby looked confused, she added, "It's an art us mermaids are taught at MUMS—that's my school.

We have to comb our hair, sing, and pay attention to our positions while sitting on slippery rocks in the sea, all at the same time. It's not easy to do!"

Their guide continued adding difficulties until finally Eros lost his balance. One by one, more team members fell out, or fell over, actually. Eventually it came down to just Porphy, Athena, Apollo, and Poseidon who were left tapping, rubbing, and nodding, plus doing other actions on top of those.

Apollo went down next. Since he was the last of his team, it meant his whole team was eliminated. Apollo took this with typical good humor, though. No big deal to him, probably, thought Poseidon. That godboy already had plenty of temples dedicated to him. He deserved them, but so did Poseidon!

Next, Porphy fell over! Awesome! Now only Athena and him were left. Just thinking about how much he wanted to win made Poseidon slowly tense up. His concentration broke, and he stumbled.

Athena wound up besting them all. Everyone congratulated her. Thetis even gave her a hug, which reminded him of how she'd hugged that nervous Chinese goddessgirl the day before. Thetis was sweet. And kinder than him. He just couldn't bring himself to offer congratulations to his biggest rival, even though he knew he should be a good sport about the loss. After all, besides the giants, Athena was who he'd most wanted to beat in the Temple Games. Now their two teams were the students' only hope of beating the giants in the overall competition!

For the three teams' next to last challenge Zeus sent a listscroll of six destinations to choose from, which the sari-robed guide handed to Athena. "As the winner of this challenge, you are entitled to pick one destination from among them," the guide told her.

Athena scanned the list. Then she called out, "We'll go to Egypt!" After being given some directions to a temple there, they were off again. Together, the students winged over the Arabian Sea, Saudi Arabia, and the Red Sea to the Egyptian temple at Karnak.

There, in a hall full of enormous columns, another guide trailed by two young servant boys met the three final teams. The guide wore a white pleated linen robe and had painted dark kohl around his eyes. He shot the giants a surprised glance, but Poseidon wasn't sure if that was because he hadn't known there would be giants in the competition or because they were dripping wet, having stomped and swum the whole way.

"You are standing in Hypostyle Hall," the guide informed the group.

"Hippo style?" Pandora piped up. "Like the animal?"

The guide shook his head, then patiently spelled the word, going on to explain that the term described a hall with many tall columns supporting its roof. "This hall's one hundred and thirty-four columns are arranged in sixteen unequal rows. Some are over sixty feet tall and are covered with paintings, sculptures, and hieroglyphics, as you can see."

As he went on, Poseidon noticed that one by one, the giants were all leaving the temple hall. That was curious. Why weren't they staying to hear the challenge? He wasn't the only one to notice. It would have been hard to miss even one humongous giant sneaking out of a room, much less five. "Where are those giants going?" the ever-curious Pandora blurted out at last.

One of the servant boys pointed north. "I heard

225

them say their mom wanted to see them at the Parthenon."

Pandora wrinkled her nose in confusion. "Pantheon? Wasn't that our first challenge?"

"The *Pantheon* is in Rome," Dionysus told her. "The giants went to the *Parthenon* in Greece."

"But we haven't even started the challenge here. Do you think they're up to something?" Pandora asked.

"Good question," Poseidon said. "I'd like to know the answer to that one too!" There were murmurs of agreement from all the other students.

"This is most irregular. The Parthenon is the location of your final challenge, so they've skipped ahead," their guide declared. "I suggest we forgo this challenge so you may join them."

Did the giants think they could race off to the last challenge and win the Temple Games unopposed?

Poseidon wondered as the teams scrambled out of the temple hall.

"Those giants are cheating *scum*," Delphinius muttered from beside him.

"Zeus won't let them get away with this, will he?" Panacea asked.

"I—I'm not sure," Athena replied, overhearing.

Poseidon could guess why she might not be sure. Zeus could be a pretty tricky character himself, so he might admire the trickiness of these giants.

"We have to stop them!" Thetis exclaimed as everyone raced outside. Poseidon grabbed her hand, and Athena grabbed onto Heracles as the members of both teams took to the air in their winged sandals.

Poseidon's heart sank as they flew toward Greece. The Parthenon was Athena's most famous temple. The one she'd been awarded for her invention of the olive. He'd avoided that place like the plague ever since she'd won (and he'd lost) the invention contest that had caused the city of Athens to be named for her. She'd know that temple inside out and would have a real advantage because of that knowledge in whatever challenge they faced there. Unless, of course, the contest was over and the giants had already won!

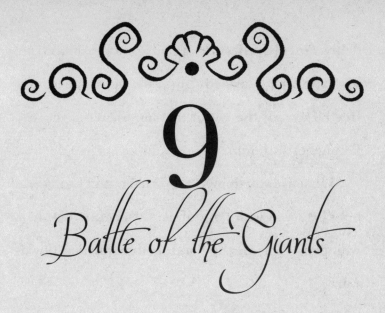

9
Battle of the Giants

Amphitrite

WORRIED THAT THOSE CHEATING GIANTS might actually win the Temple Games, Amphitrite and the other students zoomed toward Greece. Hardly a word was spoken to break the tension among them as they followed the Nile River north until it branched out into the Mediterranean Sea.

They'd been flying along for some time, when suddenly Poseidon's face whipped toward Amphitrite, his expression alarmed. Abruptly, he dropped in a freefall toward the glittering blue waters of the sea, taking her with him.

"What are you doing?" she cried out in fear, grabbing his hand with both of hers. Her turquoise hair whipped wildly in the wind as they hurtled downward.

"You haven't been in the sea for over twenty-four hours," he shouted over the wind. "Aren't you feeling landsick?"

"No!" she said in surprise.

Poseidon slowed, stopping just short of plunging them both into the Mediterranean. The silver wings at their heels fluttered, allowing them to hover just above the waves. "So you don't need to shape-shift into a mergirl?"

Amphitrite shook her head. "I don't think so. I don't feel at all landsick, isn't that weird?

"Yeah, I don't get it," Poseidon said as he took them higher again. They put on a burst of speed to catch up with the others. "I've never met a mer-person who could stay out of the sea for more than twenty-four hours without feeling sick."

Amphitrite's mind was racing as fast as they were flying. *It must be the omphalos pearl!* she thought. While she'd held it at Delphi, she remembered murmuring, "And *my* wish would be to be able to live on land *or* sea!"

The pearl had granted her wish!

She felt for it in the pocket of her scalloped chiton. Still there. If it really was allowing her to remain in shifted form without getting landsick, just think what that could mean! The rest of the pearls on the omphalos could do the same for her sisters, too, if that was the wish they chose. It was the protection they all needed. But how could she get the omphalos away from those giants?

"The truth is, I'm pretty new to shape-shifting," she admitted, sharing only part of the truth.

Poseidon raised his eyebrows. "Huh? I'd heard you were great at shifting. It's one of the reasons I invited you to be on my team."

Amphitrite paled. Was she about to be found out? She knew she should probably tell him the whole truth. That she wasn't Thetis, who actually was great at shifting. But what if he got so mad at the trick she and her sister had played on him that he left her behind in the sea? She had started to like this guy, she realized. And she didn't want him to think badly of her.

Before she could decide what to do, they caught up to the others and Harmonia shouted, "Look! Giants!"

Amphitrite glanced down. The Parthenon was below them already. She'd seen drawings of it in a scrollbook at MUMS. Gleaming white, it dominated a hill called the Acropolis, overlooking Athens, the city named for Athena. The five giants were running all around the Acropolis now, searching high and low for something.

"What in the Underworld are they looking for?" said Hades.

Seeing the students approach, Porphy pointed them out to his brothers. The five giants faced the students and braced their feet wide, as if preparing to fight. However, the students wisely hovered out of reach above the giants' heads.

Amphitrite's eyes locked onto the omphalos, which Porphy still wore as a crown. Getting anywhere near it—and its pearls—seemed impossible. Poseidon would never fly her to it. That would be too dangerous. Was there some way to make the giant take it off? she wondered.

Suddenly, Gaia's voice rumbled up from the earth. "Tell them," she demanded.

"Who's she talking to?" Amphitrite heard Pandora wonder.

The answer came a moment later when Zeus's voice boomed from the sky above them. "Students! Circumstances force me to make a new, treacherous bargain. In order to avoid waging a terrible war across many lands, Gaia and I have agreed that today's final challenge will decide more than just the winner of the games. It will determine who takes ultimate possession of the omphalos—her or me. That special stone is more powerful than you know. Without it to mark the center of the world, the earth will soon become unbalanced. The stakes have been upped. Winners take all."

"All the world, that is," Gaia's voice interrupted, laughing smugly. "Because whoever controls that hollow stone, rules the world. Including Mount Olympus. Once my boys win, all you Olympians will mooove out of MOA and we will mooove in!"

"*If* you win, that is," said Zeus. It sounded like he was gritting his teeth, barely keeping his temper in check. "And remember, no interference, Gaia. If either of us gets involved in this final round, the other team automatically wins the stone."

"Oh, sure, sure," Gaia said casually.

Amphitrite didn't trust her one bit!

"Do well, MOA teams! The fate of the world rests in your hands," Zeus said somberly. "Now Gaia and I will leave you to it."

When he stopped speaking, all the students looked stunned as they bobbed in midair, still not daring to go near the giants. But soon the five giants went back to their search.

"What's the final challenge?" Athena and Poseidon demanded at the same time. When Zeus and Gaia remained silent, everyone looked at Pheme.

She glanced up from her scroll-gadget, her face pale. Then she spoke words that rose above her as cloud letters that all could clearly read. "It's a hunt for something called the herb of invulnerability. Whoever finds it first wins for their team."

The students stared at one another blankly. "Anyone know what it looks like?" Amphitrite asked at last.

"Too bad Persephone's not here," Hades said as all the students shook their heads. "She probably would."

"I guess those cheating giants know, but they're not going to tell us," snarled Dionysus.

"It's got to be some kind of plant that makes you invulnerable—impossible to hurt or kill—" Athena began.

She broke off when Harmonia pointed into the distance, yelling, "Ye gods! More giants are coming!"

"Uh-oh. Gaia said she had a hundred sons, remember?" said Heracles.

Amphitrite turned to look and gasped. Giants were popping up all over, shaking the ground as they came running in waves. Some were dressed in armor, wielding spears. Others carried flaming torches or bags of large rocks, which they promptly launched into the air at the student teams.

"No fair!" said Delphinius.

Pheme looked up from studying her scroll-gadget, her face serious. "True, but there's nothing in the game rules that says Gaia can't add to her team. I guess Zeus never expected anything like this to happen."

"We're good fighters, but we're outnumbered. This is impossible," Poseidon declared.

Especially when a few of the students, like her, couldn't fly on their own, Amphitrite thought. Luckily, the very next second reinforcements arrived, flying in from all directions.

"Look!" she called, gesturing all around. "The other teams are back. There's Artemis and Apollo. And even Persephone . . . and everyone!" Her heart nearly burst with joy and relief to see them all.

"Dodge!" someone called out as the giants below

lobbed more rocks and began pitching spears too. The students all scattered, flying off in different directions.

"It's a free-for-all!" yelled Hephaestus. He swooped down to bean several of the giants with the silver cane he used for walking.

"Take that, you dumb giants!" shouted Ares, hurling his spear.

Though they were in terrible danger, to Amphitrite's ears they almost sounded happy to be battling the giants. She sensed Poseidon's desire to fully join in the fight alongside his immortal friends. She couldn't blame him. The defense of the world was at stake!

"Take me down to the ground," she urged him. "I'll be okay. The giants aren't really interested in me, or anyone who's not an Olympian. You guys are the ones they want to crush."

He hesitated, unsure.

"Go," she insisted. "I see Persephone down there hunting for the herb of invulnerability. While you're fighting the giants off, I'll help her."

He looked ready to argue, but then a cry for backup from Hades caught his attention and he flew her to the ground. "Shout if you need me," he said. Then he was off to join the battle in the air.

On the ground, Amphitrite joined Persephone in darting here and there to search for the herb. Soon Athena abandoned her fight with a blue-steam giant and flew over to help them.

"The plant we're looking for has got small heart-shaped leaves that glow in the dark," Persephone explained.

"It won't be dark for a while though. And we won't be able to hold off so many giants till nightfall,"

Athena said as the fight raged all around them.

Amphitrite leaped aside just in time to avoid being stomped underfoot by a giant racing past. "Is there a magic spell that could make it dark now, before actual nightfall?" she asked when she'd recovered her wits.

Persephone shook her head. "If only."

"Hey," said Athena. "I actually know someone who might be able to help us make darkness come early. C'mon!"

The goddessgirls each took one of Amphitrite's hands in theirs, and the three of them flew straight up toward the sun. When the sun's heat became almost too much to bear, Athena called out, "Greetings, Helios!"

"Helios? The sun god?" Amphitrite echoed in awed tones.

"Athena has had dealings with him before," Persephone whispered to her.

Minutes later, the god who was responsible for driving the sun across the sky each day appeared to them in his golden carriage, pulling on the reins to stop his horses. "What? I've got a schedule to keep," he demanded curtly.

"We came to ask you to drive the sun back out of the sky. Right now! It's important, I promise. Just give us ten minutes of darkness and you can drive it back into the sky again," Athena assured him. Then she explained about the herb they were trying to find and pointed out the huge battle taking place below.

As the three girls flew low over the battlefield, Helios did as Athena had asked. Within minutes, the sky darkened to black. Gasps of surprise and confusion sounded from both giant-size and student-size combatants around them.

"There!" Amphitrite called out as the girls' eyes

scanned the Acropolis. "I see a glow on the ground near the corner of the Parthenon. It's different than the glow of the giants' torches. More greenish. Could that be the herb?"

"I hope so! Let's go see!" said Persephone. They took a sharp nosedive that left Amphitrite breathless, heading for the greenish-white glow.

Athena reached the plant first. She plucked it from the ground and held it high. "The herb of invulnerability! We've found it!" But no one heard. Around them everything was loud and chaotic, as, in the darkness, the battle raged on by the light of the giants' torches.

Apollo and Artemis were pummeling Porphy with gold and silver arrows. Hephaestus was heaving volleys of rocks at another giant. Dionysus darted around whacking giants with his pinecone-tipped staff, called a thyrsos. However, no matter what the students tried, the giants just kept coming back for more.

"There are too many of them," moaned Persephone.

"And what they lack in brains, they make up for in brute strength," Athena added.

It was true. And terrible. "We have to let them know our side—the MOA side—has won. But how?" said Amphitrite. Just then she caught sight of Poseidon battling a giant with brown-steam hair.

"We'll bury you!" yelled the giant.

"Oh yeah? We'll see about that!" Poseidon yelled back. From his trident, he sent a hydraulic blast of water to carve out a deep valley below the giant's feet.

"Huh?" Before that giant knew what was happening, he sank down, down, down.

"So long!" shouted Poseidon. "Home to Mommy!

Right back into the earth you giants came from before you popped out to cause all this trouble!"

Quickly the mud flowed back in around the giant, burying him up to his eyebrows. All that remained visible was the very top of the giant's head and the brown steam flowing from it.

"He turned that giant into a volcano!" Amphitrite quipped. In spite of the danger all around them, Athena and Persephone burst out laughing.

10

Victory!

Poseidon

IT WASN'T UNTIL HELIOS HAD DRIVEN THE SUN back into the sky, turning everything bright again, that Poseidon realized how strangely dark it had been just minutes before. Now he turned from the brown-steam giant volcano he'd just created to see Heracles waging a ground battle against Porphyrion. The prince of the giants still wore the omphalos crown!

Porphy was the one to defeat! he decided. Then they could recapture the all-important omphalos that Zeus had said was more powerful than the students knew. However, even Heracles' incredible strength was no match for the big guy. Porphy had him cornered. If Poseidon attacked, he might cause the giant to fall on Heracles. That could get messy.

"Let's make a giant volcano!" Poseidon yelled to Heracles, flying closer. Porphy swung an arm trying to swat him. Poseidon winged out of reach just in time, but his trident was knocked from his hands.

Having gotten Heracles' attention, though, Poseidon pointed to the volcano he'd created with the brown-steam giant, to show the mortal boy what he had in mind. Catching on, Heracles quickly used his great strength and his club to dig a hole around Porphyrion's feet. Without his trident, Poseidon

247

wasn't much help. But he did manage to distract Porphy from what Heracles was up to by darting around him like a pesky mosquito.

"Whoa!" yelled the giant a few minutes later. Slipping and sliding, he dropped feet-first down into the enormous hole Heracles had created. In seconds, Porphy was buried all the way up to his pea-green steam!

The two boys high-fived. "Success! Giant volcano number two!" yelled Poseidon.

Seeing what the two boys had done, other airborne Olympians began heading off in different directions, taunting the giants into following. Soon, the distant sounds of digging and squelching mud could be heard as each giant was turned into a new volcano. Still more giants were led farther afield to become volcanoes in various places around the world.

Poseidon hovered a few dozen feet above the ground and stared at the green steam wafting up from the volcano Heracles had made. Then he looked around till he found Thetis. She was standing next to Athena, who was holding up a plant. He could guess what it was. The herb of invulnerability.

In his heart he knew that helping Heracles had been the right and only choice. The world had been saved and immortals would keep possession of Mount Olympus. Still, he couldn't help feeling a little sad. If he'd somehow managed to bury the prince of the giants himself and find the herb of invulnerability, then his team would have won the Temple Games. He would have earned a temple of his own. But Heracles had nailed Porphy and *he* was on Athena's team. Besides, Athena had found the herb. And that must mean that her team had won.

So, instead, his team would come in second place. He'd probably win a statue of himself in someone else's temple or something like that. Same as usual for him. Always second best, never first.

He went lower, hoping to secure the omphalos from Porphy, at least. But as he touched down, Gaia sprang from the earth to block his way.

In her true earth goddess form, she was a formidable sight. Cobwebs, small bones, and bits of moss were tangled in her mud-covered hair, and she smelled like rotting leaves, wormy tree trunks, toadstools, and dank soil. He guessed that was about right for an earth goddess, though.

"Out of my way! I am the goddess of the earth, fool! You don't think I can unbury my ooown sons?" She let out an evil cackle. But then she got a closer look at Volcano Porphy and gasped. "Nooo!

Where is it? The omphalos is *gooone!*" she wailed.

Alarmed, Poseidon went closer and saw that it was true. Suddenly, before Gaia could carry out her threat to unbury her sons, a mighty thunderbolt zapped down from the sky. There was only one god with an arm powerful enough to hurl a thunderbolt like that. *Zeus!* Poseidon jumped back. *Ka-BLAM!* The bolt caught the back of Gaia's dress and drove her deep underground into the earth she ruled. Not another peep came out of her after that!

"Congratulations, Theeny!" boomed Zeus's voice. The King of the Gods and Ruler of the Heavens shot out of the clouds in a chariot pulled by his winged horse, Pegasus. "Your team has won the Temple Games! Not to mention saved Mount Olympus and the world."

Poseidon turned to see that Athena and Persephone

were now standing nearby. He walked over to them and took a deep breath.

"Congratulations on your win," he told Athena. It was the hardest thing he'd ever done, congratulating her like that. But it was the right thing to do.

"Thanks, but Dad's got it wrong," Athena told him, shaking her head. Then she called up to the sky, "Poseidon deserves this win. He could've squashed Porphy himself, but instead he let Heracles handle it. And Thetis saw the herb first. She's on Poseidon's team."

"Nevertheless, you picked the herb of invulnerability, and your teammate Heracles buried the giant prince!" roared Zeus. "Your team won, fair and square. Tomorrow you may choose where your new temple is to be located."

Swooping lower, he landed and spoke to Poseidon.

"You have won my admiration, and the admiration of Mount Olympus and the world. An illustration of your battles with Heracles against Porphyrion will be prominently carved in Athena's new temple."

"Thank you," said Poseidon, trying to sound grateful. And he was. But still.

Then Zeus's expression drew into a frown. "Now, where is that omphalos?"

But Poseidon and Athena could only shrug. They had no clue.

11

Pearls

Amphitrite

THE OMPHALOS!" AMPHITRITE MURMURED IN awe. When Porphyrion had dropped into the earth, it had fallen from his head and rolled right to her as she hid behind the Parthenon to avoid the worst of the fighting. She stood alone now, staring at the three-foot-tall stone egg where it sat on the ground at her feet. Was it just a coincidence that the egg had come to her? she wondered. Or did it mean for her to have it—or its pearls, at any rate?

Up close she could see that she'd guessed right about this special stone. What had originally appeared to be a carved fishnet design on its surface was actually a carving of a necklace wound around and around the stone. A necklace embedded with real pearls!

She reached out, running her fingers over the lustrous, pale golden pearls and wanting to pluck them out. Did she dare? Zeus had said the omphalos was super powerful. If she took more pearls from it, what would happen?

"What do you mean, you don't know where the omphalos is?" she heard Zeus thunder from a distance away.

Amphitrite snatched back her hand and peeked around the Parthenon wall to see a group of students

255

and Zeus all standing beside the newly created green-steam volcano.

"It had better not be damaged. The omphalos's power comes from an enchanted strand of pearls carved upon it. If even one is missing, I fear it will become useless for keeping the world in balance," Zeus boomed in a troubled tone.

A chill swept through Amphitrite. What Zeus just said changed everything. It meant she would have to give the omphalos back right away. She wouldn't get to keep the pearls. Not even the one in her pocket, which she suspected had allowed her to safely shape-shift for long stretches of time. Without the pearls her sisters wouldn't get their wishes either. And she wouldn't get to hang out with these new friends she'd made. No, it was back to the sea for her. Back to being a full-time Nereid.

"It's here," she called dully. Within seconds, Zeus, Athena, Persephone, Heracles, Poseidon, and Delphinius joined her.

"Good work," Zeus commended her, brightening at the sight of the omphalos. "Let's get it back to Delphi. Heracles? Can you do the honors?" Heracles hefted the stone egg easily in his arms. He, Zeus, and Athena turned to go.

"Wait!" Amphitrite held out her fist and slowly opened it. In her palm lay the pearl from her pocket.

"Where did you get that?" asked Poseidon.

"It got caught in my sandal back in the Delphi sanctuary," she explained. "I think it's from the omphalos."

Zeus took the pearl and began to search all over the stone egg, a quizzical look on his face. "But none of its pearls are missing."

"Look again. One m-must b-be," began Amphitrite.

Then she felt herself pale and she began gasping, suddenly dizzy. "Oh no! I have to go back to the sea. I think I'm getting . . . landsick."

"Where's my trident?" yelled Poseidon, coming to her aid. When he couldn't find it right away, he picked her up and winged off, rushing her into the nearest sea.

Splash! As soon as he dunked her, Amphitrite felt fine. Shifting back to her mermaid form, she dove deep in a spiral, then returned to him, breaking the surface of the water. She gave a hard flip of her tail, splashing him.

"Fizzy! Feels good to be in the water again." Although she'd rather live on land, she'd never want to give this up completely.

He looked at her, his expression still concerned. Before he could say anything, however, two godboys flew past on their way back to MOA. Makhai tossed Poseidon's trident down to him. "Hey, your drippy-ness! Found this lying on the battlefield. Did you forget anything else? Your tubby toys and flippers maybe?" he teased.

Kydoimos laughed and glanced at Amphitrite as he hooked a thumb at Poseidon. "He's famous for them around bath time back in the dorm."

Amphitrite was dumbfounded. Her sort-of-crush played with tubby toys? And wore flippers in the bathtub? When she noticed that Poseidon's turquoise cheeks had blushed apple red, she felt an immedi-ate desire to defend him. Because so what if he liked floaties? He probably missed the sea, and they were reminders. No way she'd let these mean guys embar-rass him because of that!

"That's so adorable!" she exclaimed, clasping her

hands together. "My dad has tons of tubby toys too!" she fibbed. "And he's Nereus Of-the-Sea, the most respected merman around."

At this, Makhai and Kydoimos looked taken aback.

"It's a mer thing. You wouldn't understand," Amphitrite told them. She smiled at the two mean boys. "But maybe having a few tubby toys of your own would improve your dispositions, since they're so much fun. Think about it."

After they departed, obviously disappointed that their teasing had missed its mark, she and Poseidon both burst out laughing. Once their giggles died down, a small silence fell.

Amphitrite looked out to sea. "Well, I guess I'd better get home," she began.

"Wait!" someone called. It was Athena. She was running toward them across the shore! Heracles was behind her, carrying the omphalos in his muscled arms. Only someone with his strength could have carried a three-foot stone egg so easily. Behind them, Zeus's chariot was parked in the white sand, waiting.

Amphitrite swam to a large dark rock along the shore and pulled herself out of the water. Poseidon did the same. Quickly, she shifted back to her land legs. She was really getting the hang of the shifting spell. At least that was something.

As the two waded from the rock to shore, Athena and Heracles hurried over to join them. When the girls met, Athena held out the pearl to her. "My dad said to return this to you. We checked carefully, and none of the egg's pearls are missing."

"What? That can't be!" said Amphitrite, shaking her head. "It's the exact same color as the other pearls on the omphalos. And where else would this pearl have come from?"

Then she straightened as sudden excitement zipped through her, along with a whole new thought. Could what she was thinking possibly be true?

She looked at Zeus, who had come over to see what was going on. "Um, can we try something?" Quickly she explained what she wanted to do. Zeus was reluctant at first. The omphalos was, after all, a very important artifact not to be trifled with. Eventually, he agreed, however. Slowly, Amphitrite reached out and plucked another pearl from the omphalos. *Pop!* Immediately, a new one appeared in its place. Everyone gasped. Even the King of the Gods was surprised.

"I guess that's the omphalos's way of making sure it will always have the pearls it needs to make prophecies and keep the world from spinning out of control," said Zeus. Then he grinned big. "Good to know!"

Amphitrite gazed at him with hope in her eyes. "Do you think . . . I mean, would it be okay for me to take more pearls from it?" she dared to ask. "Like, maybe fifty of them in all? You see, that first pearl kept me from getting landsick, and I'd like to share that gift with my sisters."

"Hmm. Well," said Zeus.

"Please, Dad?" said Athena. "She helped us find the herb."

"All right," said Zeus after a minute. "I owe your dad, anyway. Nereus is a good guy."

Quickly, the two girls began plucking pearls from the egg. Each time one was removed, a new one popped up to take its place. Once they had enough, Zeus set the omphalos back in his chariot and soared off to return the stone egg to Delphi.

After scouting along the shore, Heracles found an empty clamshell to safely store Amphitrite's small pile of pearls, and Athena quickly wove her a sea-weed belt to secure the shell at her waist on her trip home. Meanwhile, Poseidon found a long strand of sea-grass and strung the pearl she'd discovered back at Delphi into a necklace she could wear.

At long last, Athena gave Amphitrite a farewell hug. Then the goddess offered her hand to Heracles, so he could fly with her.

"See you back at the Academy, Poseidon. Bye, Thetis. Nice meeting you."

Thetis. Amphitrite knew she should have said something right then. Told them the truth about who she was. But she let the moment pass. And then Athena and Heracles were gone, leaving only her and Poseidon.

12
Confidence

Poseidon

POSEIDON WALKED THETIS INTO THE WAVES. "Guess this is good-bye, then, huh?" he said as water swirled around their feet.

Thetis nodded. "Thanks for everything. It's been an adventure, and I'm really glad to have these pearls to take home to my sisters."

"Yeah, it was cool hanging out," he told her

nonchalantly. She flicked him a glance, but he didn't know what else to say.

"Okay, then. Bye," she said after a silence. Shifting back to her mermaid form, she gave a swish of her tail and dove. Poseidon watched her swim away, her golden scales gleaming brightly a few feet below the water's surface. An uncertain feeling filled him.

Hearing a series of clicks and whistles, he turned to see Delphinius. He was in dolphin form and had suddenly popped up from the sea.

"You just going to let her go?" Delphinius asked in clicks and whistles.

"Eavesdrop much?" said Poseidon, raising an eyebrow. "Where have you been, anyway?"

Delphinius transformed himself into a boy again, then stood and shrugged. "Around. Long enough to see you totally wimp out with Thetis."

"Huh? That's not true. I was just—"

"Where's your confidence, god-dude?" Delphinius butted in. "You seem to have loads of it except when it comes to her. Which can only mean one thing. You are crushing on her!"

Poseidon stared at him in consternation. Could he be right? He turned to gaze after Thetis. Her scales were barely visible now, but he could find anyone in the sea no matter where they went. He ruled it! Did he want to go after her? His heart said that he did.

He made a move to do just that, but then paused to look back at Delphinius. "Thanks, buddy. You know me better than I know myself sometimes. Glad you were on my team!" Then he added, "Why don't you come up to MOA next week? I'll show you around the place."

Delphinius's face lit up as bright as a constellation. "Really? That'd be awesome! Yeah."

"Talk later, then," said Poseidon, grinning. "I'm off to catch up with Thetis."

Within minutes, he was swimming alongside her under the sea. Surprised to see him, she let out a trill of bubbles and surfaced. They stared at each other, treading water.

"What's up?" she asked him. "I didn't expect to see you again so soon."

"I just wanted to say I'm sorry," he blurted. "I got off on the wrong foot, er, fin with you. You see, there was this Oracle-O cookie fortune back at MOA before the games began and . . . well, never mind. I'm just sorry I wasn't nicer from the beginning. Okay, Thetis?"

"Oh," she said, looking a little guilty all of a sudden. "I have something to tell you, too. Um . . . I'm not Thetis." She shot him an anxious look. "I'm actually her twin sister, Amphitrite."

His jaw dropped. Then he just couldn't help it. He started laughing.

"What's so funny?" she asked, frowning at him as her arms swept back and forth in the water.

Finally, he told her about the Oracle-O cookie and how he'd almost invited her—the real Amphitrite—to join his team instead of Thetis. "The cookie said Thetis could outshine me, so when I thought you were her, I was worried you'd try to outdo me somehow."

"No way!" she said, flipping her tailfin so it almost splashed him.

"Way. But you totally supported me and everyone else. And you were kind of . . . nice. It was mega confusing, let me tell you, *Amphitrite*," Poseidon said. Trying out her name for the first time, he decided he liked it.

Her cheeks turned a little pink. Was it because he'd sort of admitted he liked her? Poseidon wondered.

"I hope I didn't hurt anyone or cause trouble by pretending to be Thetis," she said quickly. "I was only hoping to travel and . . . I wanted to pretend to be this adventurous, amazing, *shape-shifting* person for a while. The kind of person Zeus might invite to go to MOA. Someone like Thetis, who really is pretty fizztastic. Only she has no interest in leaving the sea, so we made a deal. I came to the games in her place."

They'd drifted to a rock sticking up from the sea, and she grabbed onto it so they could talk more easily. "I'm sorry about the temple prize," she said softly. "I know how much you wanted it."

Poseidon smiled wryly, grabbing the other side of the rock. "Pretty obvious, huh?" Then he sighed.

"I thought winning a temple would prove my worth, but maybe that was kind of lame." His gaze caught hers, turquoise meeting turquoise. "You may have pretended to be someone you're not, but in a way, I was too, I guess. Pretending to be secure and confident when I don't really feel that way. It was stupid to feel threatened by a dumb Oracle-O cookie."

"You have a good heart," she said earnestly. "I really believe that. You did the right thing, helping Heracles end the battle."

He looked out to sea, then back at her, nodding. "It wasn't easy to congratulate Athena, though. I really did want my own temple. And I didn't get it. That's kind of hard to take, but I'll get over it."

Thetis, no, *Amphitrite* considered him, appearing to weigh something in her mind. Then, seeming to reach some decision, she said, "Come with me, okay?"

Turning, she sped off in the direction of the Undersea. After a moment's hesitation, he followed, and the two of them swam side by side.

"Where are we going?" he asked, bubbles streaming off behind them as he spoke.

"You'll see," she told him, her eyes sparkling.

13

Surprise!

Amphitrite

An hour later, they saw it glistening ahead deep underwater. A magnificent palace of gleaming gold.

"There it is," Amphitrite told Poseidon, pointing. "What I brought you to see."

His eyes widened in wonder. "What is this place?" he asked, moving closer to examine it. "It's amazing!

I'm god of the sea. Why didn't I know about it?"

"Because it's a surprise. For you," she told him. "Makes sense your temple would be under the sea, right?"

"A *temple*? For me?" he repeated, obviously astounded. "But who built it?"

"Who builds temples?" she said, shrugging as she beamed at him. "An immortal's fans, of course. In this case all the creatures of the sea. They've— we've—been building this place for years now. To show you that we of the sea are all behind you. We know you have our backs. That you protect us and are always thinking of our welfare. And we appreciate it."

"Whoa," he said, grinning a little. "I never knew mers thought so highly of me."

"We do. But I know you won't let it go to your head, right?" She laughed, then went on earnestly. "This palace is your temple. It's a place all sea creatures will be able to gather to celebrate you. And you can meet here to talk sea-business with my dad, and leaders from other watery realms too. It's not finished yet, but with everyone happily contributing the time and materials they can, it won't take too much longer."

She showed him a mosaic of tiles that depicted him larger than life, riding three hippocampi through tumultuous waves, his trident raised high in battle. "Last year, all my sisters and I made this mosaic from bits of shells we collected."

He smiled at it in genuine delight. "It's perfect. Totally perfect."

"That carving Zeus said you won in the Temple Games would look great right next to it," she added. They explored the palace a little more, discussing and admiring various features.

Then, tossing his blond hair out of his eyes with flick of his head, Poseidon smiled at her through the water. He had the best smile ever! she thought.

"So about coming to school at MOA," he said. "If you really want to, I'll support your request. And I think Athena will, too. We have pull with the big guy. Principal Zeus, I mean."

Amphitrite's eyes went wide, a thrill shooting through her. She'd already decided she was going to face her dad with the truth about her love of land. If Principal Zeus did invite her to attend MOA, she knew her dad wouldn't refuse the honor. And that would be so great!

"I do want to go to MOA," she assured Poseidon, nodding. "More than anything."

After they explored the palace for a while longer, they said their good-byes and swam off, him to MOA and her to the Undersea. Feeling *fin*tastically happy, Amphitrite sped like an arrow through the water. She had fifty tiny gifts to deliver. Well, forty-nine.

She touched the lustrous pearl that dangled from the sea-grass necklace Poseidon had made for her and which now encircled her throat. As long as she had the pearl, she'd be safe on land or in the sea for any length of time. She could choose where to go, what to do, and who to be. And the very best part was that her sisters would soon be able to do the same. Once they had the legendary magical pearls in their possession, she wouldn't have to worry about them getting landsick ever again.

With a flip of her fin, Amphitrite dove even deeper into the blue waters of the Aegean, heading for home with the greatest gift ever close to her heart. The gift of hope—hope of an invitation to return as a student at Mount Olympus Academy. *Fizzy!*

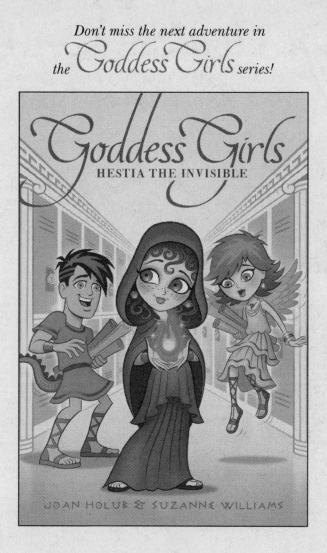

Goddess Girls

READ ABOUT ALL
YOUR FAVORITE GODDESSES!

**#17 AMPHITRITE
THE BUBBLY**

**#16 MEDUSA
THE RICH**

**#15 APHRODITE
THE FAIR**

**#14 IRIS
THE COLORFUL**

**#13 ATHENA
THE PROUD**

**#12 CASSANDRA
THE LUCKY**

**#11 PERSEPHONE
THE DARING**

**#10 PHEME
THE GOSSIP**

**#1 ATHENA
THE BRAIN**

**#2 PERSEPHONE
THE PHONY**

**#3 APHRODITE
THE BEAUTY**

**#4 ARTEMIS
THE BRAVE**

**#5 ATHENA
THE WISE**

**#6 APHRODITE
THE DIVA**

**#7 ARTEMIS
THE LOYAL**

**THE GIRL GAMES:
SUPER SPECIAL**

**#8 MEDUSA
THE MEAN**

**#9 PANDORA
THE CURIOUS**

EBOOK EDITIONS ALSO AVAILABLE

From Aladdin
KIDS.SimonandSchuster.com